Folk Tales from Italy

West Agora Int

West Agora Int

Timisoara 2024

WEST AGORA INT S.R.L.

All Rights Reserved

Copyright © WEST AGORA INT 2024

F.T. Weaver

Folk Tales from Italy

Volume 1

Enchanted Legends of Magic, Miracles, and Mythical Heroes from Italian Folklore

Folk Tales from Italy Copyright © 2024 West Agora Int

Published by West Agora Int
Edited by West Agora Int
Cover Art by West Agora Int

Discover a world where magic, miracles, and myth collide in the heart of Italy's rich storytelling tradition.

In Folk Tales from Italy: Enchanted Legends of Magic, Miracles, and Mythical Heroes from Italian Folklore, embark on an unforgettable journey through the mystic hills and ancient villages of Italy, where every shadow hides a secret and every whisper carries the promise of enchantment.

Meet La Befana, the kind-hearted witch who soars through the night sky, delivering gifts to children on the Epiphany. Dive into the shimmering depths with Colapesce, the half-man, half-fish who sacrifices everything to save Sicily from disaster. Feel the courage of Saint Agatha, whose faith defies all odds, and dance to the rhythm of the Tarantella, born from the bite of a venomous spider and transformed into a joyous celebration of life.

These are tales of wonder and woe, of laughter and loss—each one a doorway into a realm where the impossible becomes reality. From the magic of a talking vine that reveals hidden truths to the cursed power of a ring that grants every wish with a dangerous twist, these stories will captivate your imagination and stir your soul.

Whether you're a lover of folklore, a seeker of ancient wisdom, or simply someone who yearns for tales that transport you to another time and place, this collection is your gateway to the spellbinding world of Italian legends. Let these stories enchant you, inspire you, and remind you of the timeless power of a well-told tale.

Turn the page, and let the magic begin.

Dedication

To the storytellers of old,
whose voices have carried these tales through the
centuries,
and to the dreamers and seekers,
who find magic in the everyday.
May these stories continue to inspire and ignite the
imagination
of all who turn their pages.

With gratitude and admiration,
F.T. Weaver

TABLE OF CONTENTS

La Befana.. 11

The Tale of Colapesce.. 23

The Legend of Saint Agatha.................................. 35

The Talking Vine...51

The Tale of the Laughing Apple............................ 73

The Legend of the Tarantella................................92

The Legend of the Olive Tree...............................107

The Magic Ring...121

Epilogue... 140

La Befana

In a small, rustic village nestled in the rolling hills of Italy, there lived an old woman named Befana. She was a familiar figure in the village, with her bent back, weathered face, and eyes that sparkled like stars despite her age. She lived alone in a tiny stone cottage at the edge of the village, where she kept a tidy home and spent her days sweeping the floors, baking delicious treats, and tending to her small garden. Befana was known for her industrious nature and her skill in keeping her house spotless—so much so that people often joked she spent more time sweeping than sleeping.

Befana had no family of her own, and while she was not unfriendly, she preferred solitude, finding comfort in her simple routines. The villagers would occasionally see her at the market, where she would exchange her baked goods for supplies, but most of the time, Befana remained in her cottage, her broom always in hand.

One evening, as Befana was sweeping the front of her cottage under the twinkling stars, she heard a commotion coming from the village road. It was unusual to hear anything other than the wind or the rustling of leaves at this hour, so Befana paused and looked up. Through the darkness, she saw a small group of travelers approaching, their figures silhouetted against the moonlit sky.

As they drew nearer, Befana could see that the travelers were richly dressed and carried an air of importance about them. They were the Three Wise Men, or Magi—Caspar, Melchior, and Balthazar—who had been following a bright star in the sky, guiding them to the newborn King of the Jews. The Magi had traveled from distant lands, bearing precious gifts of gold, frankincense, and myrrh for the Holy Child.

Befana, intrigued but cautious, stood at her doorway as the Wise Men stopped in front of her cottage. The tallest of them, with a flowing beard and kind eyes, addressed her.

"Good evening, kind woman," he said. "We are weary travelers on a sacred journey, following the star that leads us to the Christ Child. We have come far, but the night grows cold, and we seek shelter and guidance. Might you assist us in finding our way?"

Befana, taken aback by their request, hesitated. She had heard tales of this child, born to bring light into the world, but she had never been one for grand tales or prophecies. Her life was small, simple, and predictable—she liked it that way.

After a moment, she replied, "I am but a simple woman. I know nothing of kings or stars. But if you need rest, my home is humble, yet warm. You are welcome to stay."

The Wise Men accepted her offer with gratitude, and Befana ushered them into her cottage. As she prepared a modest meal, the Wise Men spoke of their journey, the star they followed, and the child they sought to honor. Befana listened quietly, her heart stirred by their words, but still, she felt distant from the grand purpose that drove these men.

After they had eaten, the Magi thanked Befana for her hospitality and prepared to continue their journey. Before leaving, they once again invited her to join them, to come and see the child who was destined to change the world.

But Befana shook her head, clinging to her broom as if it were a lifeline. "No, I cannot go. I have too much to do here. My house needs sweeping, and my work is never done."

The Wise Men nodded, understanding that not everyone was called to the same path. They bid her farewell and continued on their way, leaving Befana alone once more.

Yet, as the night wore on and Befana sat by her fire, something inside her began to change. The thought of a child, born to bring hope to the world, gnawed at her. She had never had children of her own, and the idea of missing out on such a momentous event began to weigh heavily on her heart. What if this child was truly as special as the Wise Men had said? What if, by staying behind, she was missing her only chance to be part of something greater than herself?

Befana tossed and turned in her bed, unable to sleep. The thought of the Christ Child filled her mind, and she felt a deep sense of regret for not having joined the Wise Men on their journey.

Finally, she could bear it no longer. She leaped out of bed, grabbed her broom, and gathered the best of her baked goods—figs, dates, honey cakes, and other treats. She wrapped them in a cloth and set out into the cold night, determined to find the Wise Men and the child they sought.

Befana hurried along the path the Wise Men had taken, her heart pounding with urgency. The night was cold, and her breath hung in the air like a mist, but she was driven by a newfound purpose. She would find the child, and perhaps, by offering her simple gifts, she could make up for her earlier hesitation.

The bright star that had guided the Wise Men still shone in the sky, and Befana used it to guide her steps. But as she traveled through the night, she began to realize that she had no idea where the Wise Men had gone. The world beyond her village was unfamiliar to her, and the roads stretched on endlessly into the darkness.

Still, Befana pressed on, asking every traveler she encountered if they had seen the Wise Men or knew where the Christ Child might be. But no one could help her. Some had seen the star, but none knew where it led. Others had heard of the child, but his whereabouts were a mystery. Befana's determination wavered as the night grew longer, and her legs grew weary.

By dawn, Befana found herself at a crossroads. She stood there, looking up at the fading star with a heavy heart, realizing she was lost. The Wise Men were nowhere to be found, and the child she sought seemed impossibly far away.

Exhausted and discouraged, Befana sank down by the side of the road. She had failed. The regret that had driven her to leave her cottage now weighed on her like a stone, and tears welled up in her eyes.

But as she sat there, she heard the sound of a child's laughter in the distance. Befana wiped her eyes and looked around, hoping against hope that she had finally found the child. She got up and followed the sound, her heart lifting with renewed hope.

The laughter led her to a small village, where she saw children playing in the streets. They were laughing and running, their faces bright with joy. Befana stood at the edge of the village, watching them, and something inside her softened. The sight of the happy children filled her with warmth, and she realized that while she might never find the Christ Child, she could still bring joy to these children.

Befana reached into her bundle and took out the treats she had prepared for the child. She called out to the children, who quickly gathered around her, curious about the old woman with the kind eyes. Befana handed out the figs, dates, and honey cakes, and the children accepted them with delight.

As she watched them eat, Befana felt a sense of peace she had not known in years. She might not have found the child, but she had found a way to share her love and kindness. And in doing so, she realized she had found a new purpose.

From that day forward, Befana continued her journey every year on the night before Epiphany. She would travel from village to village, bringing gifts to children, hoping that one day, she might still find the Christ Child. And though she never did, she became a beloved figure in every town she visited, known as the kindly old woman who brought joy to children on Epiphany Eve.

Over time, the legend of La Befana grew, and she became an integral part of the Italian Epiphany tradition. Children would leave their shoes out by the fireplace or their beds, hoping that La Befana would visit during the night and fill them with sweets and small gifts. If the children had been good, they would wake to find their shoes filled with treats; if they had been naughty, they might find a lump of coal instead.

And so, La Befana's story continues to be told to this day, a tale of a simple woman who found her way into the hearts of children everywhere, embodying the spirit of love, generosity, and redemption.

Cultural Significance and Facts about La Befana

The story of La Befana is deeply rooted in Italian culture and has become an integral part of the country's holiday traditions, particularly surrounding the celebration of the Epiphany on January 6th. The tale of La Befana, the kindly old woman who delivers gifts to children on the night before Epiphany, is much more than just a charming folk story; it embodies the values of generosity, redemption, and the blending of ancient pagan and Christian traditions. La Befana is not merely a character from folklore; she represents a unique cultural phenomenon that offers insight into Italy's rich and diverse cultural heritage.

The Epiphany and La Befana's Role

In Christian tradition, the Feast of the Epiphany commemorates the visit of the Three Wise Men, or Magi, to the Christ Child. It marks the end of the Twelve Days of Christmas and is considered a significant event in the Christian liturgical calendar. The Epiphany is celebrated with various customs and rituals across the Christian world, but in Italy, it holds a particularly special place, thanks in large part to the figure of La Befana.

La Befana is often depicted as an elderly woman, somewhat resembling a witch, with a tattered shawl, a long skirt, and a broomstick that she rides through the night. However, unlike the sinister witches of other European traditions, La Befana is a benevolent figure. On the night of January 5th, she flies from house to house, delivering gifts to children who have been good and leaving lumps of coal for those who have been naughty. In this way, she serves a similar role to that of Santa Claus in other cultures, but with distinct characteristics that make her uniquely Italian.

The name "Befana" itself is believed to be a corruption of the Italian word "Epifania," which is the Italian name for the Epiphany. Over time, the name evolved, and so did the story of La Befana, blending elements of Christian and pre-Christian traditions into a uniquely Italian figure.

Pagan Origins and Christian Integration

The roots of the La Befana tradition can be traced back to pre-Christian pagan rituals that were prevalent in ancient Italy. Before the advent of Christianity, the Romans celebrated the new year with a festival called Saturnalia, which honored the god Saturn. This festival, held in late December, involved the giving of gifts, feasting, and merrymaking, much like modern Christmas and New Year's celebrations. During Saturnalia, it was also common for people to exchange small presents, particularly among children, which may have influenced the later development of the gift-giving aspect of La Befana's tradition.

Moreover, the figure of La Befana is believed to have connections to the ancient Roman goddess Strenia, a deity associated with the new year, purification, and well-being. Strenia was honored with gifts of fruits and sweets during the new year celebrations, and her name has given rise to the Italian word "strenna," which means a gift or present given during the holiday season. The transformation of Strenia into La Befana is an example of how pagan deities and rituals were gradually assimilated into Christian traditions, resulting in the blending of cultural and religious practices.

As Christianity spread across Italy, the Church sought to integrate these pagan customs into Christian celebrations, creating a smooth transition for converts. The figure of La Befana was adapted to fit the new Christian context, and her story was tied to the Epiphany, a feast day that already had deep religious significance. In this way, La Befana became a symbol of the Christianization of Italy, representing the convergence of old and new beliefs.

La Befana's Symbolism and Cultural Values

La Befana's story is rich in symbolism, reflecting important cultural values that resonate deeply with Italian society. At its core, the tale of La Befana is about redemption and the idea that it is never too late to change one's path or to make amends for past mistakes. Befana's decision to set out on her journey to find the Christ Child, despite her initial refusal, highlights themes of repentance and the pursuit of a better life. This aspect of the story is particularly poignant in a culture that places great emphasis on personal responsibility, forgiveness, and the possibility of redemption.

Furthermore, La Befana embodies the value of generosity, which is central to Italian culture. Her actions—bringing gifts to children and spreading joy—mirror the Italian emphasis on family, community, and the importance of giving. In Italy, the holiday season is a time of coming together, sharing meals, and showing kindness to others, and La Befana's tradition of gift-giving reflects these values.

The dual nature of La Befana's gifts—sweets for the good and coal for the naughty—also carries an important cultural message. It reinforces the idea of moral accountability, teaching children that their actions have consequences. This concept is deeply embedded in Italian family life, where children are often encouraged to reflect on their behavior and strive to be their best selves.

Additionally, La Befana's broom, while often associated with witches, carries a different symbolism in this context. In Italian culture, the broom is not just a tool for cleaning; it is also a symbol of sweeping away the old to make way for the new. La Befana's journey on her broom can thus be seen as a metaphor for renewal and the hope that each new year brings.

Modern Celebrations and Regional Variations

Today, the tradition of La Befana is celebrated throughout Italy, though the customs surrounding her vary by region. In many parts of the country, children hang stockings by the fireplace or place their shoes out, hoping that La Befana will fill them with treats such as chocolates, candies, and small toys. In some regions, particularly in rural areas, children might also find fruit or nuts in their stockings, reflecting the more modest origins of the tradition.

In the town of Urbania in the Marche region, La Befana is celebrated with a grand festival known as the "Festa della Befana." This event draws visitors from all over Italy and features parades, performances, and the appearance of a life-sized Befana who hands out gifts to children. Urbania is sometimes referred to as the "home" of La Befana, and the town takes great pride in this annual celebration, which has become one of the most well-known Epiphany events in Italy.

In Rome, Piazza Navona hosts a popular market in the days leading up to the Epiphany, where vendors sell Befana-themed toys, sweets, and decorations. This market, known as the "Mercato della Befana," is a beloved tradition for both locals and tourists, offering a festive atmosphere where people can shop for last-minute holiday gifts and enjoy the holiday spirit.

Another regional variation can be found in Venice, where a traditional Befana regatta takes place on the Grand Canal. In this event, participants dress up as La Befana and race in boats, creating a playful and uniquely Venetian twist on the celebration.

In recent years, the image of La Befana has even been commercialized, with her figure appearing on holiday decorations, greeting cards, and souvenirs. However, despite the commercialization, the essence of the tradition remains strong, as La Befana continues to be a beloved symbol of the Epiphany and the values it represents.

La Befana in Popular Culture and Beyond

The story of La Befana has also made its way into popular culture, both within Italy and internationally. She has appeared in various books, films, and television programs, often depicted as a wise, kindly figure who embodies the spirit of the holiday season. In Italian literature, La Befana is sometimes portrayed as a solitary figure who finds joy in her mission to bring happiness to children, reflecting the importance of altruism and community in Italian culture.

Internationally, La Befana has captured the imagination of those outside Italy as well, particularly among Italian diaspora communities. In countries with significant Italian populations, such as the United States, Canada, and Argentina, La Befana is often celebrated alongside other Christmas and New Year traditions, helping to preserve a sense of cultural identity among Italian immigrants and their descendants.

La Befana's story also serves as a reminder of the universal themes of kindness, generosity, and the power of myth to shape cultural identity. While her tale is uniquely Italian, the values she *represents resonate with people from all walks of life, making her a timeless figure in the pantheon of holiday legends.*

Conclusion

La Befana is more than just a character from a folk tale; she is a symbol of Italian culture, history, and tradition. Her story, which blends ancient pagan rituals with Christian beliefs, offers a window into the rich tapestry of Italian life and the enduring power of myth to convey important cultural values. Through her annual journey on the night before Epiphany, La Befana continues to bring joy to children and adults alike, reminding us of the importance of generosity, redemption, and the simple pleasures of life. As long as her story is told, La Befana will remain a cherished part of Italy's cultural heritage, a testament to the enduring power of folklore to connect us with our past and guide us into the future.

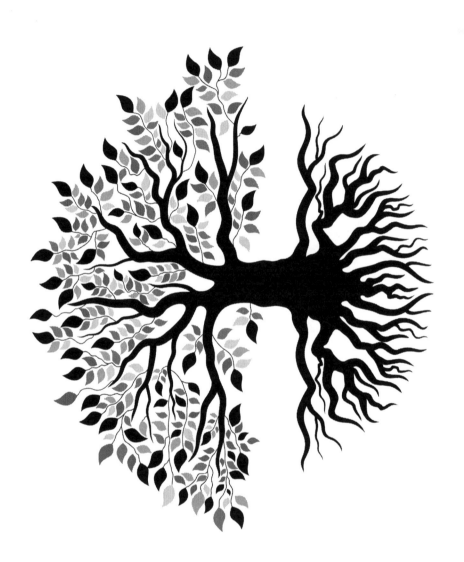

The Tale of Colapesce

In the sun-drenched island of Sicily, where the rugged mountains meet the sparkling Mediterranean Sea, there lived a young boy named Cola. From a very young age, it was clear that Cola was different from the other children in his seaside village. While they played on the shore, Cola was irresistibly drawn to the water, spending hours swimming in the sea, exploring its depths with a natural ease that amazed everyone around him.

As Cola grew older, his connection to the sea deepened. The villagers began to speak of him with awe, saying that he could stay underwater for hours and dive deeper than anyone else. Some even whispered that Cola was part fish, a child of the sea as much as of the land. Because of his incredible abilities, he came to be known as Colapesce, a name that combined his own with the Italian word for fish—pesce.

Colapesce's fame spread quickly across Sicily. He would dive deep into the ocean, bringing back pearls, ancient coins, and other treasures from shipwrecks long forgotten. He knew the underwater caves and currents as well as he knew the streets of his village, and the sea seemed to hold no secrets from him. Colapesce's affinity for the ocean was so great that people began to believe he had been blessed—or perhaps enchanted—by the sea gods themselves.

Despite his growing renown, Colapesce remained humble and kind. He was always willing to help the fishermen by finding their lost nets or guiding them through treacherous waters. The sea was his domain, and he felt a deep responsibility to protect it and those who relied on it.

It was not long before tales of Colapesce's remarkable abilities reached the ears of the King of Sicily. The King was a man of great curiosity and ambition, and he was intrigued by the stories of the boy who could swim like a fish and explore the ocean's depths. He decided that he must meet this Colapesce and see for himself if the stories were true.

The King summoned Colapesce to his court, and although Colapesce preferred the company of the sea to that of men, he respected the King's authority and agreed to go. When Colapesce arrived at the royal palace, the King welcomed him warmly, but with a hint of skepticism in his voice.

"Colapesce," the King began, "I have heard many tales of your adventures beneath the sea. They say you can dive deeper and stay underwater longer than any man. Is this true?"

Colapesce, with the humility that had endeared him to his village, replied, "Your Majesty, I have spent my life in the sea. It is my home, and I know its ways better than most. But there is always more to discover beneath the waves."

The King, intrigued but unconvinced, decided to test Colapesce's abilities. "If you are truly as skilled as they say, I have a task for you," the King said. "There is a golden cup, lost long ago in the depths of the sea. Many have tried to retrieve it, but none have succeeded. If you can bring me this cup, I will believe the stories of your talents."

Without hesitation, Colapesce accepted the challenge. The sea was not something he feared; it was where he belonged. With the King and his court watching from the shore, Colapesce dove into the deep blue waters, disappearing beneath the surface.

As Colapesce descended into the depths, the sunlight gradually faded, and the water grew colder. But he swam with confidence, knowing that the ocean held no danger for him. He passed through underwater valleys and over ancient shipwrecks, his eyes scanning the seabed for any sign of the lost cup.

After a time, he saw it—a flash of gold among the rocks. Colapesce swam closer and found the cup, half-buried in sand and covered in a thin layer of algae. He grasped it firmly and began his ascent, swimming swiftly back to the surface.

When Colapesce emerged from the water, holding the golden cup aloft, the King and his court gasped in amazement. The King himself was astonished, for he had doubted that anyone could retrieve the cup from such depths. "You truly are remarkable, Colapesce," the King said, his voice filled with admiration. "But now, I have another task for you, one that is of even greater importance."

The King went on to explain that there were legends about the very foundations of Sicily. It was said that the island rested on three great pillars, deep beneath the sea. These pillars, according to the stories, supported the entire weight of the island, keeping it from sinking into the ocean. The King, ever curious and concerned for the safety of his kingdom, wanted Colapesce to dive down and examine these pillars to ensure that they were still strong and intact.

Colapesce agreed, understanding the gravity of the task. The safety of Sicily depended on these pillars, and if there was any truth to the legends, he needed to confirm it. Without delay, he prepared for the dive that would take him deeper into the sea than he had ever gone before.

With the King's new challenge weighing heavily on his mind, Colapesce prepared himself for the most important dive of his life. The task was daunting, but Colapesce was determined to fulfill his duty, not just to the King, but to the island of Sicily itself, which had always been his home. He took a deep breath and dove into the sea once more, plunging into the depths where few had ever dared to venture.

As Colapesce descended, the familiar embrace of the sea surrounded him. The water grew darker and colder as he swam deeper and deeper, leaving behind the sunlit surface world. He passed through underwater forests of swaying kelp and over sunken ruins from ancient civilizations long forgotten. The sea was silent here, save for the distant echoes of the deep.

Colapesce pushed on, knowing that he had to reach the very bottom of the sea where the legendary pillars were said to stand. His heart beat steadily, and his eyes were sharp, scanning the murky depths for any sign of these fabled supports. The deeper he went, the more the pressure of the water weighed on him, but Colapesce was undeterred. He was driven by a sense of responsibility and a love for his island that gave him strength.

Finally, after what felt like an eternity of swimming, Colapesce saw something massive looming in the darkness. As he approached, he realized that he had found them—the three great pillars that were said to hold up the island of Sicily. They were enormous, rising from the seabed like ancient monoliths, their surfaces encrusted with barnacles and seaweed.

Colapesce swam around the pillars, marveling at their size and the way they seemed to anchor the island above to the very depths of the earth. But as he inspected them more closely, a deep unease began to settle in his heart. The first two pillars he examined were strong and solid, their foundations firmly planted in the ocean floor. But when he reached the third pillar, Colapesce's heart sank—it was cracked and crumbling.

The pillar, though still standing, showed signs of severe damage. Large fissures ran along its length, and pieces of stone had already broken away and fallen to the seabed below. It was clear to Colapesce that this pillar could not support the weight of Sicily for much longer. If it failed, the entire island could collapse into the sea, taking with it the people, villages, and everything Colapesce held dear.

Colapesce knew that he had to act quickly. He had to return to the surface and warn the King about the danger that Sicily faced. But as he began his ascent, a troubling thought crossed his mind—there was no way to repair such a massive structure, and the island's fate seemed inevitable. Colapesce paused, floating in the dark water, and considered the gravity of the situation.

He realized that there was only one solution, one way to save Sicily from disaster. It was a solution that required a sacrifice, a sacrifice that only he could make. Colapesce, the boy who had been born with the sea in his veins, knew that he could not abandon his island to its fate. The only way to prevent the pillar from collapsing was to hold it up himself, to become the support that Sicily needed.

With a heavy heart, Colapesce made his decision. He swam back down to the base of the cracked pillar and positioned himself beneath it. Using all his strength, he pressed his hands and shoulders against the massive stone structure, steadying it as best he could. The weight of the island above bore down on him, but Colapesce held firm, determined to keep Sicily safe.

As he braced himself against the pillar, Colapesce felt a strange calm wash over him. He knew that he would never return to the surface, that he would never again see the sun, the sky, or his beloved village. But he also knew that his sacrifice was necessary, that by giving his life, he was ensuring the safety and future of his island and its people.

The sea, which had always been Colapesce's home, now became his final resting place. He became one with the ocean, his body and spirit merging with the water that had always embraced him. The legend says that Colapesce remained there, holding up the pillar, his strength preventing the island from sinking into the sea.

Back on the surface, the King and his court waited anxiously for Colapesce to return. Hours passed, and then days, but there was no sign of the boy. The King, realizing the enormity of what must have happened, mourned the loss of Colapesce and recognized the great sacrifice that had been made.

In time, the story of Colapesce spread across Sicily and beyond. He became a symbol of selflessness, devotion, and the deep connection between the people of Sicily and the sea. The legend of Colapesce was passed down through generations, a tale of a boy who gave his life to save his island, ensuring that Sicily would remain standing for centuries to come.

Cultural Significance and Facts about The Tale of Colapesce

The Tale of Colapesce, or Cola Pesce, is a cornerstone of Sicilian folklore, deeply embedded in the cultural identity of Sicily and the broader Italian peninsula. This story, which has been passed down through generations, transcends the simple narrative of a boy with extraordinary abilities; it embodies profound themes of sacrifice, the human relationship with nature, and the mystique of the sea. The legend of Colapesce has not only shaped local customs and beliefs but also offers insight into the island's history, geography, and the resilience of its people.

Origins and Variations of the Tale

The story of Colapesce likely has its origins in medieval folklore, with its first known versions appearing as early as the 12th century. It draws on a rich tapestry of myths and legends that existed in Sicily long before the island became part of modern Italy. Like many folk tales, The Tale of Colapesce has numerous variations, each reflecting the particular cultural and historical context of the time and place in which it was told.

In some versions of the story, Colapesce is described as a young boy who is part human and part fish, an element that echoes ancient myths of mermaids, tritons, and other sea creatures. In other tellings, he is simply a human with extraordinary abilities, capable of diving to the deepest parts of the sea and holding his breath for incredible lengths of time. Regardless of the variation, the core of the story remains the same: Colapesce's deep connection to the sea, his selfless act of sacrifice to save Sicily, and his transformation into a legendary figure who symbolizes the island's enduring strength.

The tale has also been influenced by the blending of Christian and pagan traditions, a common feature in many Southern Italian and Sicilian stories. While the character of Colapesce might have originally been rooted in pre-Christian mythology, the story was later adapted to fit into the Christian worldview, which emphasized themes of martyrdom and self-sacrifice.

Symbolism and Themes in the Tale

At its heart, The Tale of Colapesce is a story about sacrifice and the deep, almost spiritual connection between the people of Sicily and the sea that surrounds them. Colapesce's willingness to give up his life to save the island reflects the importance of selflessness and duty in Sicilian culture. This theme resonates particularly strongly in a society that has historically faced numerous challenges, from natural disasters to invasions by foreign powers. Colapesce's sacrifice symbolizes the resilience and tenacity of the Sicilian people, who have endured through centuries of hardship.

The sea, which plays a central role in the story, is both a source of life and a symbol of the unknown. For Sicilians, who have always lived in close proximity to the ocean, the sea represents both opportunity and danger. It provides sustenance through fishing and trade, but it is also unpredictable and can bring devastation in the form of storms and earthquakes. Colapesce's deep affinity with the sea and his ultimate decision to merge with it underscores the dual nature of this relationship: one of respect, fear, and reverence.

The three pillars on which Sicily is said to rest are another significant symbol in the tale. These pillars can be seen as representing the island's geographical and cultural foundations, its stability, and its connection to the earth. The damaged pillar that Colapesce discovers is a metaphor for the vulnerabilities that all societies face—be they political, economic, or environmental. By holding up the pillar, Colapesce becomes the guardian of Sicily's future, ensuring that the island remains safe and secure.

In addition to these overarching themes, the story of Colapesce also touches on the concept of transformation. Colapesce begins as a human boy, but through his connection with the sea and his ultimate sacrifice, he transforms into a legendary figure, almost a demi-god, whose presence is felt even after he has disappeared. This transformation reflects the idea that individuals can transcend their ordinary lives and achieve greatness through acts of courage and selflessness.

Historical and Cultural Context

The tale of Colapesce is more than just a story; it is a reflection of Sicily's complex history and the cultural influences that have shaped the island. Sicily has been a crossroads of civilizations for millennia, with Phoenicians, Greeks, Romans, Arabs, Normans, and others leaving their mark on the island. Each of these cultures brought their own myths, legends, and beliefs, which blended together to create the rich tapestry of Sicilian folklore.

During the Middle Ages, when the earliest versions of Colapesce's tale likely emerged, Sicily was a melting pot of different cultures and religions. The island was a key battleground during the Norman conquest, and the subsequent rulers sought to consolidate their power by promoting stories that emphasized loyalty, sacrifice, and divine protection. The story of Colapesce, with its themes of self-sacrifice for the greater good, would have resonated strongly in this context, serving both as a moral lesson and a source of comfort for a population that was often caught in the crossfire of larger geopolitical struggles.

In addition to its historical significance, the tale of Colapesce also reflects the geographical reality of Sicily. The island is located in, a seismically active region, and earthquakes and volcanic eruptions have been a constant threat throughout its history. The idea that Sicily is held up by three pillars beneath the sea can be seen as a way for the island's inhabitants to make sense of the natural forces that shape their lives. Colapesce's sacrifice to support the damaged pillar is a symbolic representation of the islanders' resilience in the face of these natural threats.

The Legacy of Colapesce in Modern Culture

Today, the legend of Colapesce remains àn integral part of Sicilian culture. The story is taught to children as part of their education in local folklore, and Colapesce is often depicted in literature, art, and popular media. His image is a familiar one in Sicily, where he is celebrated as a local hero and a symbol of the island's enduring connection to the sea.

In literature, Colapesce has inspired countless retellings and adaptations. Italian poets and writers, such as Giovanni Meli and Luigi Capuana, have explored the legend in their works, using it as a vehicle to express themes of identity, sacrifice, and the relationship between humans and nature. The tale has also been the subject of scholarly analysis, with historians and folklorists examining its origins, variations, and cultural significance.

Colapesce's story has even found its way into popular culture. In the 20th and 21st centuries, the legend has been adapted into films, animated series, and even songs. These modern interpretations often emphasize the environmental themes of the story, with Colapesce being portrayed as a protector of the sea and a symbol of ecological awareness. In this way, the tale continues to evolve, remaining relevant to contemporary audiences while preserving its traditional roots.

In Sicily, the story of Colapesce is celebrated in various local festivals and cultural events. In the town of Messina, which is often identified as Colapesce's home, the tale is commemorated with special performances and reenactments. These events not only honor the legend but also serve to reinforce the values that Colapesce represents—courage, selflessness, and a deep respect for the natural world.

Conclusion

The Tale of Colapesce is more than just a piece of folklore; it is a powerful narrative that captures the essence of Sicilian culture and identity. Through the story of a boy who sacrificed himself to save his island, the legend conveys themes of duty, sacrifice, and the enduring relationship between humans and the natural world. Colapesce's legacy lives on in the hearts and minds of the Sicilian people, a testament to the power of storytelling to preserve cultural values and connect generations.

As long as the story of Colapesce is told, it will continue to serve as a reminder of the importance of selflessness, the strength of community, and the profound connection between Sicily and the sea that surrounds it. In this way, Colapesce remains a guardian of the island, not just in legend, but in the cultural consciousness of Sicily itself.

The Legend of Saint Agatha

I n the ancient city of Catania, nestled at the foot of the formidable Mount Etna, there lived a young woman whose faith and courage would forever change the course of history. Her name was Agatha, and she was born into a noble and wealthy family during the early part of the 3rd century, a time when Christianity was still a persecuted faith under the rule of the Roman Empire. From a young age, Agatha was known for her piety, purity, and devotion to God, qualities that set her apart from her peers.

Agatha's parents, who were devout Christians themselves, nurtured her faith and instilled in her a deep love for God. As she grew older, Agatha made a solemn vow to dedicate her life to Christ, choosing to remain a virgin as a symbol of her unwavering commitment to her faith. Her beauty, both physical and spiritual, was renowned throughout Catania, and many suitors sought her hand in marriage. However, Agatha gently but firmly refused all proposals, explaining that her heart belonged solely to God.

Despite the growing Christian community in Catania, the

Roman Empire, under the rule of Emperor Decius, was fiercely opposed to the new religion. Christians were often subjected to persecution, torture, and even death if they refused to renounce their faith and worship the Roman gods. It was in this perilous time that Agatha's faith would be put to the ultimate test.

Word of Agatha's beauty and devotion reached the ears of Quintianus, the Roman governor of Sicily. Quintianus was a man of power and ambition, known for his ruthless enforcement of the empire's laws. When he learned of Agatha's refusal to marry and her commitment to Christianity, he saw an opportunity to both fulfill his desires and further his standing with the emperor by making an example of her. Quintianus decided that he would force Agatha to renounce her faith and become his wife, believing that no woman could resist his power.

Quintianus sent for Agatha, commanding that she be brought to his palace in Catania. When Agatha arrived, she stood before the governor with a calm and serene demeanor, her heart filled with trust in God. Quintianus was struck by her beauty and grace, but he was also determined to bend her to his will.

"Agatha," Quintianus said, "you are as beautiful as they say. You deserve to live in luxury, to enjoy the pleasures of life, and to be honored as my wife. Renounce this foolish faith of yours, and I will give you everything you desire."

But Agatha was resolute. She looked Quintianus in the eye and replied, "I am a servant of Christ, and my heart belongs to Him alone. No earthly riches or power can tempt me to abandon my faith."

Quintianus, unused to being defied, felt a surge of anger. But he hid his frustration behind a smile and continued to press her. He offered her wealth, status, and protection, promising that she would never want for anything if she would only renounce her faith. Yet, Agatha remained steadfast, refusing every offer with a gentle but firm "no."

Realizing that persuasion would not work, Quintianus' demeanor darkened. He ordered Agatha to be taken to a brothel, hoping that the shame and humiliation would break her spirit. For a month, she was subjected to the lewd advances of men and the scorn of women, but Agatha's faith did not waver. She prayed constantly, asking God to give her the strength to remain pure in body and soul.

To the amazement of all, Agatha emerged from the brothel unscathed, her chastity and faith intact. The brothel's mistress, who had been tasked with corrupting Agatha, was so moved by her strength and devotion that she even began to question her own life choices. Furious at his failure, Quintianus ordered Agatha to be brought back to his palace. He was determined to break her by any means necessary.

When Agatha stood before Quintianus again, she was even more resolute than before. The governor, seeing that she could not be swayed by temptation, decided to resort to cruelty. He ordered that Agatha be imprisoned and tortured until she renounced her faith. He hoped that the pain and suffering would cause her to submit to his will.

Agatha was thrown into a dark, cold cell, where she was left to languish without food or comfort. But even in the depths of her suffering, she did not lose hope. She continued to pray, finding strength in her unwavering faith. The days in the prison were long and brutal, but Agatha's spirit remained unbroken.

One day, after weeks of confinement, Quintianus ordered that Agatha be brought to the torture chamber. There, in a display of his cruelty, he commanded that her breasts be cut off—a punishment meant to symbolize the destruction of her purity and womanhood. Agatha endured the torture with incredible fortitude, her mind focused on the love of Christ. According to the legend, after this brutal act, she was returned to her cell, where she prayed for God's mercy and healing.

That night, a miraculous event occurred. As Agatha lay in her cell, weak from pain and blood loss, a vision of Saint Peter appeared before her. The apostle, surrounded by a radiant light, spoke words of comfort to Agatha and miraculously healed her wounds. When the guards came to check on her the next morning, they were astonished to find her completely healed, her strength and beauty restored.

The news of Agatha's miraculous recovery spread quickly, and many began to believe that she was truly favored by God. But Quintianus, blinded by his anger and pride, refused to be swayed. Instead of releasing her, he ordered that Agatha be subjected to even greater tortures, determined to crush her spirit once and for all.

After hearing of Agatha's miraculous recovery, the people of Catania were in awe, whispering among themselves that she must be divinely protected. Some began to question the authority of Quintianus, wondering if his cruelty might bring divine retribution. But the Roman governor, enraged by his inability to bend Agatha to his will, was consumed by a desire to assert his power and crush her defiance.

Determined to make an example of Agatha, Quintianus ordered that she be brought before him once more. When Agatha appeared in the governor's court, she was pale but serene, her wounds miraculously healed, her spirit as strong as ever. Quintianus, however, saw only a challenge to his authority, and his eyes burned with cold fury.

"Agatha," he said, his voice laced with malice, "you have defied me at every turn, and now even your wounds have been healed by some trickery. But know this: no one defies the power of Rome and lives. Renounce your faith, or you will suffer worse than you can imagine."

Agatha stood tall, her gaze unwavering as she met Quintianus' glare. "My faith is my life," she replied calmly. "I fear nothing, for Christ is my strength. You may destroy my body, but my soul belongs to God, and nothing you do can take that from me."

Her words, spoken with quiet conviction, only fueled Quintianus' rage. He ordered that Agatha be subjected to a series of tortures designed to break her will. She was dragged back to the torture chamber, where she was beaten, burned, and racked, her body subjected to unimaginable pain. But through it all, Agatha never wavered, her prayers rising above the cries of agony.

According to the legend, even as she suffered, Agatha was sustained by her deep faith. She believed that her suffering was a test, a way to prove her devotion to Christ, and she embraced it with a sense of peace that baffled her tormentors. The soldiers who carried out the tortures were struck by her resilience, and some of them even began to question the righteousness of their actions. They whispered among themselves that perhaps this woman truly was under the protection of God, for no ordinary person could endure such torment and remain unbroken.

Despite her endurance, Agatha's body was weakened by the constant torture. But each night, as she lay in her cell, bruised and battered, she prayed for strength. And each morning, she awoke with renewed resolve, ready to face whatever horrors

Quintianus had in store for her. The governor, growing increasingly desperate to break her, resorted to even more brutal measures.

One day, Quintianus ordered that Agatha be dragged across a bed of burning coals and sharp shards of pottery. The cruel intention was to inflict unbearable pain and humiliation, hoping that the physical and psychological torment would finally force her to submit. But as the guards carried out the order, something extraordinary happened.

As Agatha was dragged across the coals, the ground beneath her began to shake violently. The people of Catania, who had gathered to witness the spectacle, cried out in fear as the earth trembled beneath their feet. The shaking grew stronger, and soon it became clear that this was no ordinary earthquake—it was a sign, a divine intervention. The mountain itself, Mount Etna, the great volcano that loomed over Catania, seemed to be responding to the injustice inflicted upon the innocent young woman.

The crowd watched in awe as the coals beneath Agatha cooled and the flames died down, leaving her body unscathed. The onlookers, many of whom had been silent witnesses to her torment, began to murmur among themselves that Agatha was indeed a saint, protected by God's power. Even some of the Roman soldiers, who had been tasked with carrying out Quintianus' orders, were struck with fear and reverence, dropping their weapons and falling to their knees.

Quintianus, however, refused to be moved by these miraculous signs. His pride and desire for control blinded him to the truth that was so clear to everyone else. He ordered that Agatha be returned to her cell, determined to find another way to break her. But the people of Catania, now emboldened by the signs they had witnessed, began to speak out against the governor's actions, calling for Agatha's release.

Locked in her cell once more, Agatha's strength began to wane. She was exhausted from the days of torture, and her body could no longer bear the suffering. But even as her physical strength faded, her faith remained unshaken. She knew that her time on earth was drawing to a close, and she accepted it with grace, offering her life to God as a final act of devotion.

On February 5, 251 AD, after enduring days of unspeakable suffering, Agatha breathed her last breath. As she lay dying, it is said that a great calm descended over Catania, as if the entire city were mourning the loss of its most faithful daughter. Agatha's death was not the end of her story, but the beginning of her legacy as a revered saint and protector of Catania.

After her death, the people of Catania took Agatha's body and buried her with great reverence. They knew that she had died a martyr, and they began to pray to her for protection and intercession. Soon, stories of miracles began to spread—people who prayed at her tomb were healed of their ailments, and the city itself seemed to be under her watchful care.

The most famous of these miracles occurred the following year, when Mount Etna erupted violently, threatening to destroy Catania. The people, fearing for their lives, rushed to Agatha's tomb and took her veil, a relic that had covered her body. They carried the veil to the edge of the city, holding it up as a shield against the advancing lava.

Incredibly, the lava flow stopped just short of the city, as if an invisible hand had held it back. The people of Catania believed that it was Saint Agatha herself who had intervened to save them, and from that moment on, she was venerated as their patroness and protector. The annual festival of Saint Agatha, held every February, became one of the most important religious events in Sicily, drawing thousands of pilgrims who came to honor the saint and seek her intercession.

Saint Agatha's legacy extends far beyond Catania. She became one of the most venerated saints in the Christian tradition, her story of faith and martyrdom inspiring countless believers throughout the centuries. Churches were built in her honor, not only in Sicily but across Italy and Europe, and her name became synonymous with purity, courage, and steadfast faith.

Today, Saint Agatha's story continues to be told, a testament to the enduring power of faith and the strength of the human spirit in the face of persecution. Her legend is a reminder that even in the darkest of times, the light of faith can shine brightly, offering hope and inspiration to all who hear it.

Cultural Significance and Facts about The Legend of Saint Agatha

The Legend of Saint Agatha is one of the most revered and enduring stories in the Christian tradition, particularly in Sicily, where she is venerated as the patron saint of Catania and a symbol of faith, courage, and resilience. Her story, rooted in historical events and enriched by centuries of devotion and folklore, offers deep insights into the cultural, religious, and social fabric of Sicily and the broader Christian world. The tale of her martyrdom during the Roman Empire and the subsequent miracles attributed to her have made Saint Agatha a powerful figure in both religious practice and cultural identity.

Historical Context and Origins

Saint Agatha was born in Catania, Sicily, around 231 AD, during a period when Christianity was still a persecuted religion under Roman rule. The Roman Empire, particularly under the Emperor Decius, was marked by intense efforts to suppress the burgeoning Christian faith, which was seen as a threat to the traditional Roman religious and social order. Christians were often subjected to brutal persecution, including torture and execution, if they refused to renounce their faith and worship the Roman gods.

Agatha's story is set against this backdrop of religious persecution. According to tradition, she was a young noblewoman of great beauty and piety who had dedicated her life to God, vowing to remain a virgin as a sign of her devotion. Her refusal to marry or to abandon her faith made her a target for the Roman governor of Sicily, Quintianus, who sought to force her into submission.

The events leading to Agatha's martyrdom reflect the broader context of the Roman Empire's efforts to maintain control over its territories and suppress any challenges to its authority. Her resistance to Quintianus' demands and her subsequent suffering highlight the tensions between the Christian community and the Roman state, making her story a powerful example of the conflict between faith and imperial power.

Symbolism and Themes in the Legend

The story of Saint Agatha is rich with symbolism and themes that resonate deeply within the Christian tradition and beyond. Her steadfastness in the face of torture, her miraculous healing, and her ultimate martyrdom are seen as manifestations of divine grace *and the power of faith.*

Martyrdom and Sacrifice: At the heart of Saint Agatha's story is the theme of martyrdom. In Christian theology, martyrdom is the ultimate act of faith, a willingness to suffer and die rather than renounce one's beliefs. Agatha's refusal to submit to Quintianus, despite the horrific tortures inflicted upon her, exemplifies the Christian ideal of bearing witness to the truth of the Gospel, even unto death. Her martyrdom is a profound testament to the belief that spiritual integrity and loyalty to God are worth more than life itself.

Purity and Chastity: Saint Agatha's vow of virginity is central to her story. In the early Christian church, virginity was often associated with spiritual purity and a complete dedication to God. Agatha's commitment to this vow, despite the pressures and temptations she faced, underscores the value placed on chastity as a symbol of moral and spiritual strength. Her resistance to Quintianus' advances and her subsequent torture, particularly the mutilation of her breasts, highlight the connection between physical purity and spiritual integrity. This aspect of her story has made Saint Agatha a patron saint for those seeking protection of their purity and for women suffering from breast diseases.

Divine Intervention and Miracles: The miracles associated with Saint Agatha's story, such as her miraculous healing by Saint Peter and the stopping of Mount Etna's lava flow by her veil, are key elements of her legend. These miracles serve to confirm her sanctity and the idea that those who suffer for their faith are rewarded with divine protection. The stopping of Mount Etna's eruption in particular has solidified her status as a protector of Catania and the surrounding regions, and it is a miracle that is still celebrated annually in the festival held in her honor.

Resilience and Faith: Agatha's story is also a powerful narrative of resilience in the face of suffering. Despite the brutal tortures she endured, Agatha remained unshaken in her faith. This resilience is a key aspect of her legacy, inspiring countless believers to persevere through their own trials with the same steadfast faith that she demonstrated. Her endurance under torture, and her ultimate victory through martyrdom, embody the Christian belief that faith can overcome even the greatest suffering.

Saint Agatha's Cult and Patronage

After her death, Agatha quickly became one of the most venerated saints in Christianity, particularly in Sicily and Southern Italy. Her tomb in Catania became a site of pilgrimage, and many miracles were attributed to her intercession. Over time, her cult spread throughout the Christian world, and she was invoked for protection against fire, earthquakes, and volcanic eruptions—dangers that were, and still are, very real in her native Sicily.

Patron Saint of Catania and Beyond: Saint Agatha's most prominent role is as the patron saint of Catania. Her story is deeply intertwined with the identity of the city, and her protection is invoked not only against natural disasters like the eruptions of Mount Etna but also in times of personal and communal crisis. The people of Catania view Saint Agatha as their protector, and her image is prominently displayed in homes, churches, and public spaces throughout the city.

In addition to Catania, Saint Agatha is also the patron saint of a number of other cities and regions, particularly in Italy. Her intercession is sought by those who suffer from breast cancer or other breast-related ailments, and she is often invoked by women who have been victims of sexual assault or abuse. Her story, which *emphasizes the triumph of spiritual strength over physical violence, resonates deeply with those seeking protection and healing.*

The Festival of Saint Agatha: The Feast of Saint Agatha, celebrated from February 3rd to 5th, is one of the largest and most important religious festivals in Sicily, and indeed in the entire Catholic world. The festival is a vibrant expression of devotion and community, drawing hundreds of thousands of pilgrims and visitors to Catania each year.

The celebrations include processions, prayers, and the veneration of relics, particularly the veil that is said to have stopped the lava flow from Mount Etna. The festival is a time of great joy and communal solidarity, as the people of Catania come together to honor their beloved patroness. The centerpiece of the festival is the procession of the statue of Saint Agatha, which is carried through the streets of Catania on a silver carriage known as the "fercolo." The procession is accompanied by prayers, hymns, and the lighting of thousands of candles, symbolizing the light of faith that Saint Agatha represents.

In addition to its religious significance, the festival of Saint Agatha also has a strong cultural component. It is a time when traditional Sicilian foods, such as the famous "minnuzze di Sant'Agata" (small, breast-shaped pastries filled with sweet ricotta), are prepared and shared among families and communities. These pastries, which commemorate the torture Agatha endured, are a unique example of how her story has been integrated into the local culture and cuisine.

Saint Agatha in Art and Iconography

Saint Agatha has been a popular subject in Christian art and iconography for centuries. She is often depicted holding her severed breasts on a platter, a reference to the torture she endured. This depiction, while shocking to modern sensibilities, is a powerful symbol of her martyrdom and the spiritual strength that enabled her to endure such suffering.

In addition to this common image, Saint Agatha is also frequently portrayed with the palm of martyrdom, a crown of flowers, and a veil. The palm is a traditional symbol of Christian martyrs, representing victory over death, while the crown and veil emphasize her purity and dedication to God. These elements of her iconography reinforce the central themes of her story—martyrdom, purity, and divine protection.

Throughout history, Saint Agatha has been depicted by some of the greatest artists in the Christian tradition. Renaissance painters such as Raphael, Caravaggio, and Titian have all portrayed her, each bringing their own interpretation to her story. These works of art have not only contributed to the spread of her cult but have also helped to shape the way she is remembered and venerated.

In Sicily, many churches are dedicated to Saint Agatha, and they house some of the most important relics and artworks associated with her. The Cathedral of Catania, where her relics are enshrined, is the most significant of these, serving as the focal point of the annual festival and a major site of pilgrimage throughout the year.

The Continuing Legacy of Saint Agatha

The legacy of Saint Agatha extends far beyond the borders of Sicily. As one of the most venerated early Christian martyrs, her story has inspired generations of believers around the world. Her name is included in the Canon of the Mass in the Roman Catholic

Church, placing her among the most honored saints in the Christian tradition.

In addition to her religious significance, Saint Agatha's story continues to resonate with contemporary audiences, particularly in the context of discussions about gender, power, and violence. Her refusal to submit to Quintianus' advances, and her subsequent torture and martyrdom, are powerful symbols of resistance to oppression and the triumph of spiritual strength over physical coercion. For many, she represents the ultimate example of a woman who remained true to her beliefs in the face of overwhelming odds.

In recent years, Saint Agatha has also been embraced as a symbol of the fight against breast cancer. Her story, which involves the mutilation of her breasts, has been reinterpreted in a modern context as a source of inspiration for women battling this disease. Many organizations dedicated to breast cancer awareness and research invoke her name, and her feast day has become a time for special prayers and initiatives in support of those affected by the disease.

Conclusion

The Legend of Saint Agatha is a powerful narrative that has shaped the religious and cultural landscape of Sicily and the broader Christian world. Her story, rooted in historical events and enriched by centuries of devotion and folklore, embodies themes of faith, sacrifice, and resilience that continue to inspire believers today. As the patron saint of Catania and a symbol of purity and courage, Saint Agatha's legacy lives on in the hearts of those who honor her, and her story remains a testament to the enduring power of faith in the face of adversity. Whether invoked in prayer, *celebrated in festivals, or depicted in art, Saint Agatha continues to be a beacon of hope and a source of strength for countless people around the world.*

The Talking Vine

In a remote village nestled in the rolling hills of Italy, there was a vine unlike any other. This vine, which grew over an ancient stone wall on the edge of the village, was not famous for the sweetness of its grapes or the abundance of its fruit. No, this vine was known for something far more mysterious and unsettling—it could talk.

The vine was an ancient thing, its twisted roots burrowed deep into the earth, and its leaves thick and dark green. No one knew exactly how old it was or who had planted it, but it had been there for as long as anyone in the village could remember. The vine's ability to speak was not a constant thing; it did not chatter away like a parrot or tell stories like a human. Rather, it would speak only when approached by someone with a burning question or a deep, unresolved worry. And when it did speak, its voice was soft and whispering, like the rustle of leaves in the wind.

The villagers had learned to approach the vine with both reverence and caution. They believed that the vine had the power to reveal secrets, answer questions, and even foretell the future. But these revelations often came with a price. The vine's words were not always easy to hear, and its truths could be harsh and unforgiving. Over the years, the vine had become both a source of wisdom and a cause for fear among the villagers. Some sought it out in times of desperation, while others avoided it, fearing what they might learn.

The origins of the vine's powers were the subject of much speculation. Some said that it had been enchanted by a powerful sorcerer long ago, who had imbued it with the ability to see into the hearts and minds of men. Others believed that the vine was connected to the earth itself, drawing its knowledge from the deep roots that stretched far beneath the village. Whatever the truth, the vine had become an integral part of the village's lore, its presence woven into the fabric of their lives.

One day, a stranger arrived in the village. He was a traveler, a man who had wandered far and wide in search of knowledge and wisdom. His journey had taken him through many lands, and he had heard countless stories and legends. But when he heard of the talking vine, his curiosity was piqued. He had never encountered anything like it before, and he decided that he must see it for himself.

The villagers were wary of the stranger, as they were of all outsiders. They were a close-knit community, and they guarded their secrets closely. But the stranger was persistent, and eventually, he learned of the vine's location. One evening, as the sun dipped low in the sky and cast long shadows across the village, the stranger made his way to the edge of the village, where the vine grew over the old stone wall.

The vine was as the villagers had described it—ancient, twisted, and strangely alive. The stranger could feel its presence, a subtle but undeniable energy that seemed to emanate from the dark green leaves. He approached the vine cautiously, unsure of what to expect.

The stranger had many questions—questions about his past, his future, and the choices he had made along the way. But as he stood before the vine, he realized that there was one question above all others that weighed on his mind. It was a question that had haunted him for years, and one that he had never been able to answer. He hesitated for a moment, then stepped closer to the vine, his heart pounding in his chest.

"Tell me," the stranger whispered, his voice barely audible, "what is the truth that I seek?"

For a long moment, there was silence. The vine's leaves rustled gently in the evening breeze, but it did not speak. The stranger began to wonder if the stories had been just that—stories, with no truth to them at all. But then, just as he was about to turn away, the vine spoke.

Its voice was soft and eerie, like the sigh of the wind through the trees. "The truth," the vine whispered, "is hidden in the choices you have made and the ones you have yet to make. The path you seek lies not in the past, but in the future."

The stranger frowned, his mind racing as he tried to make sense of the vine's words. "What do you mean?" he asked, his voice trembling slightly. "I don't understand."

"The truth is not a single answer, but a journey," the vine replied. "You will find it not in what you have done, but in what you will do. The choices you make will reveal the truth, but be warned—once known, the truth cannot be forgotten."

The stranger felt a chill run down his spine. He had expected a simple answer, something that would provide clarity and direction. But the vine's words were cryptic, leaving him with more questions than answers. He stood in silence, pondering the implications of what he had heard.

Finally, the stranger spoke again. "If the truth is in my choices, then what should I choose? How can I know which path to take?"

The vine's leaves rustled again, as if in thought. "The path you choose is yours alone," it whispered. "But remember this—every choice has a consequence, and every truth has a price. Choose wisely, and be prepared to face the truth that you find."

The stranger stood in silence, the vine's words echoing in his mind. He knew that the vine had given him the answer he sought, but it was not the answer he had expected. It was a warning, a reminder that the pursuit of truth was not without its dangers.

As the sun set and the village fell into darkness, the stranger turned away from the vine and walked back toward the village. He carried with him the weight of the vine's words, knowing that the choices he made from this point forward would shape his future in ways he could not yet foresee.

But the stranger was not the only one affected by the vine's revelations. The next day, whispers began to spread through the village—whispers of secrets revealed, of truths that could not be ignored. The vine's words had set in motion a series of events that would soon change the village forever.

The stranger's encounter with the talking vine left him deeply unsettled. The vine's cryptic words played over and over in his mind as he returned to the village. He had come seeking clarity, yet he felt more confused than ever. The vine had spoken of choices and consequences, of a truth that once revealed could not be forgotten. It was a warning that weighed heavily on his heart, but it was also a challenge—a challenge to confront the unknown and face whatever truths lay ahead.

The next morning, the stranger walked through the village

with a sense of unease. The villagers, who had been cautious and reserved around him before, now seemed even more distant. He could feel their eyes on him as he passed, and he sensed that they were whispering among themselves. The vine's influence had spread beyond his own encounter; its words had begun to seep into the fabric of village life, stirring up secrets that had long been buried.

As the day wore on, the stranger noticed that the atmosphere in the village had changed. Conversations were hushed, and the villagers seemed to avoid each other's gaze. There was an air of tension, as if everyone was holding their breath, waiting for something to happen. The stranger knew that the vine's revelations were beginning to take their toll.

Later that afternoon, a commotion broke out in the village square. The stranger, drawn by the noise, hurried to see what was happening. A crowd had gathered around two men who were arguing heatedly, their voices raised in anger. The stranger recognized them as brothers, well-respected members of the community. He listened as their argument grew more intense, the words they exchanged filled with bitterness and accusation.

"You lied to me!" one of the brothers shouted, his face red with fury. "All these years, you've kept this secret from me! How could you do this? How could you betray your own family?"

The other brother, his expression a mix of guilt and defiance, tried to defend himself. "I did what I had to do! It was for the good of the family, for the good of the village! I never meant to hurt you, but you have to understand—some things are better left unsaid."

The crowd murmured uneasily, their eyes darting between the two brothers. The stranger felt a chill run down his spine as he realized what was happening. The vine had revealed a secret, a hidden truth that had festered beneath the surface for years. And now, that truth had come to light, tearing apart the bond between the two brothers and casting a shadow over the entire village.

As the argument escalated, the stranger noticed that other villagers were beginning to exchange nervous glances. It was clear that the vine's revelations had not been limited to the two brothers. Whispers of other secrets, other truths, began to ripple through the crowd. Some people exchanged harsh words, while others looked away in shame or fear. The village, once a close-knit community, was beginning to unravel under the weight of the vine's truths.

That evening, as the sun set and the village settled into an uneasy silence, the stranger found himself drawn back to the edge of the village where the vine grew. He stood before it, his heart heavy with the knowledge that the vine's power was greater than he had imagined. It was not just a source of wisdom or guidance; it was a force that could shape the lives of those who sought its counsel, for better or for worse.

The stranger hesitated, unsure if he should approach the vine again. He had come to the village seeking answers, but the answers he had found were not the ones he had expected. The vine's words had set in motion a chain of events that could not be undone, and the stranger felt a deep sense of responsibility for what had happened.

As he stood there, the vine's leaves rustled in the evening breeze, and the soft, whispering voice spoke once more. "The truth is a double-edged sword," it murmured. "It can cut through lies and deception, but it can also wound those who wield it. Some truths are best left in the shadows, hidden from the light."

The stranger bowed his head, understanding the weight of

the vine's words. He had sought the truth, but he had not considered the cost. The village was now grappling with the consequences of secrets revealed, and there was no way to undo what had been done.

In the days that followed, the tension in the village grew. The vine's revelations had opened old wounds and brought hidden grievances to the surface. Long-held grudges and buried resentments bubbled up, causing rifts between friends and families. The once-peaceful village was now a place of suspicion and discord, and the stranger could feel the growing sense of unease.

Some villagers, desperate to know more, began visiting the vine themselves, seeking answers to their own questions. But each new revelation seemed to only deepen the divisions within the community. The vine's truths were powerful, but they were also dangerous, and the villagers began to realize that the answers they sought could bring more harm than good.

The stranger, too, felt the pull of the vine's power. He had more questions, more uncertainties, and the temptation to seek further guidance was strong. But he also knew that each encounter with the vine carried a risk, a risk that he was no longer sure he wanted to take. The village was in turmoil, and he feared that any further revelations might push it to the brink of destruction.

One night, unable to sleep, the stranger wandered through the village, lost in thought. He passed by homes where families once close were now divided by the vine's revelations. He heard whispers in the dark, voices filled with regret, anger, and fear. The village was on the edge of something irrevocable, and the stranger knew that the vine's influence was at the heart of it all.

Finally, he found himself once again standing before the

vine. The night was still, and the moon cast a pale light over the ancient leaves. The stranger stared at the vine, torn between the desire for answers and the fear of what those answers might bring.

"I have one last question," he whispered, his voice barely audible in the night air. "What is the cost of knowing the truth?"

The vine remained silent for a long moment, and the stranger wondered if it would answer at all. But then, the soft, whispering voice spoke once more, and its words sent a chill through his heart.

"The cost of knowing the truth is the burden of carrying it," the vine whispered. "The truth can be a heavy load, one that cannot be set down once it is picked up. It changes you, shapes you, and it can never be forgotten. Are you prepared to bear that burden, or will you walk away?"

The stranger felt a deep sense of unease. The vine's words resonated with a truth he had not wanted to face—that some things, once known, cannot be undone. He realized that the village's turmoil was not just the result of the vine's revelations, but also of the villagers' inability to cope with the truths they had uncovered.

He turned away from the vine, his mind filled with the weight of its words. The village was at a crossroads, and the choices they made from this point forward would determine their future. The stranger knew that his presence had stirred things up, but he also knew that he could not leave without seeing things through to the end.

As he walked back to the village, he resolved to help the villagers find a way forward, to reconcile the truths they had uncovered with the lives they now had to live. It would not be easy, but the stranger believed that there was still hope, that the vine's truths, though painful, could lead to healing and understanding if approached with care.

The days that followed were fraught with tension as the village continued to wrestle with the truths revealed by the talking vine. The stranger watched as the once-close-knit community became fractured, with neighbors eyeing each other with suspicion and old friendships strained to the breaking point. It was as though the vine had unearthed not just hidden truths, but also buried resentments and long-forgotten wrongs.

But the stranger had not given up hope. He believed that the village could find a way to heal, to rebuild the trust that had been shaken. He began speaking to the villagers one by one, encouraging them to confront the truths they had learned and to seek understanding rather than allowing their fears to fester.

He visited the two brothers who had quarreled so bitterly in the square, sitting with them late into the night as they recounted their grievances. It was not easy, and at times their anger threatened to boil over again, but slowly, the stranger helped them see that their bond as family was stronger than the secrets that had been exposed. They spoke of their shared memories, of the times they had supported each other, and eventually, they agreed to forgive and move forward together.

In another home, the stranger found a woman who had learned a painful truth about her husband's past. She had withdrawn into herself, struggling to come to terms with the revelation. The stranger listened as she poured out her heart, speaking of her love for her husband and the sense of betrayal she felt. He gently reminded her that everyone has a past, and that love is sometimes about accepting the flaws and mistakes of those we hold dear. With time, she found the strength to confront her husband, and together they began the difficult process of rebuilding their relationship.

Throughout the village, the stranger's efforts began to bear fruit. Conversations that had been steeped in anger and bitterness gradually turned to ones of reconciliation and forgiveness. The villagers started to realize that while the vine's revelations had been painful, they also offered an opportunity to grow, to address the issues that had been simmering beneath the surface for years.

But even as the village slowly began to heal, the stranger knew that his work was not yet done. There was one final task that remained—one final question that needed answering. The vine had shown its power to reveal truths, but the stranger wanted to understand the true nature of that power. He needed to know whether the vine's revelations were a force for good or if they held a darker purpose.

One evening, as the sun dipped low and the village settled into a quiet calm, the stranger made his way back to the edge of the village where the vine grew. The air was cool, and the sky was streaked with the colors of twilight. The vine seemed to sense his approach, its leaves rustling softly in the breeze, as if waiting for him.

The stranger stood before the vine, gathering his thoughts. He had learned much since his first encounter, and he had seen the impact of the vine's words on the village. But there was still so much he did not understand. He knew that this would be his final visit, his last chance to uncover the vine's true nature.

He took a deep breath and spoke. "Vine, I have seen the power of your words. You reveal the truth, but that truth has brought both pain and healing to this village. I must know—what is your purpose? Do you serve to help those who seek you, or is there something more that drives you?"

The vine remained silent for a moment, and the stranger wondered if it would answer him at all. But then, the familiar whispering voice returned, carrying with it a sense of ancient knowledge and wisdom.

"My purpose," the vine whispered, "is to reveal what is hidden, to bring light to the shadows that dwell in the hearts of men. I do not choose the truths I reveal; I simply speak what is already known, but not yet understood. The truth is neither good nor evil—it simply is. How it is used, how it is received, that is for those who seek it to decide."

The stranger listened intently, his mind turning over the vine's words. "But why," he asked, "do you reveal these truths? What do you hope to achieve?"

The vine's leaves rustled again, as if in thought. "I reveal the truth because it is my nature," it replied. "I am a mirror, reflecting the desires, fears, and hopes of those who come to me. Some truths bring healing, others bring pain, but all are part of the journey each must take. The truth can be a burden, but it can also be a path to freedom."

The stranger nodded slowly, beginning to understand. The vine was not a malevolent force, nor was it a benevolent one. It was simply a conduit for the truths that already existed within the hearts of those who sought it. The vine's power lay in its ability to reveal these truths, to bring them to the surface where they could no longer be ignored.

"But what of those who cannot bear the truth?" the stranger asked, his voice tinged with concern. "What happens to those who are destroyed by what they learn?"

The vine's voice was softer now, almost tender. "Not all truths are easy to bear," it whispered. "But even the hardest truths can lead to growth, to understanding. Those who are destroyed by the truth are often those who refuse to accept it, who cling to the shadows rather than stepping into the light. The truth can be a painful teacher, but it is also a guide, leading each person toward their own destiny."

The stranger stood in silence, absorbing the vine's words. He realized that the vine was not to be feared, but rather respected. It was a force of nature, neither good nor evil, but essential to the human experience. The vine offered knowledge, but it was up to each individual to decide what to do with that knowledge.

As the last light of day faded and the stars began to twinkle in the night sky, the stranger knew that his time in the village was coming to an end. He had found the answers he sought, and he had helped the villagers come to terms with the truths that had been revealed. There was nothing more he could do.

The next morning, the stranger prepared to leave the village. The villagers, who had once been wary of him, now saw him off with gratitude and respect. They had learned much from his guidance, and they were ready to continue their journey toward healing and understanding. The village was still scarred by the truths that had been exposed, but there was a sense of hope in the air—a belief that they could move forward, stronger and wiser than before.

As the stranger walked away from the village, he glanced back one last time at the vine. Its leaves shimmered in the morning light, and for a moment, he thought he heard the soft whisper of its voice carried on the wind. But the words were lost in the breeze, and the stranger continued on his way, content in the knowledge that he had played his part.

The village would never forget the time when the vine spoke, revealing the secrets and truths that had long been hidden. And while the vine remained a source of mystery and wonder, the villagers had learned to approach it with respect, understanding that the truth, while powerful, was also something to be handled with care.

Over time, the village healed. The brothers who had quarreled became close once more, their bond stronger for having faced their past. The woman who had struggled with her husband's secret found peace in forgiveness, and their love deepened. The stranger's influence lingered, and the villagers often spoke of the lessons they had learned during that fateful time.

And so, the vine continued to grow on the ancient stone wall, its leaves thick and green, its roots burrowed deep into the earth. It remained there, waiting for those who would come with questions, seeking answers to the mysteries of their own hearts. The vine would continue to speak, revealing the truths that lay hidden, offering guidance to those who dared to listen.

But those who sought the vine's counsel knew that the truth was not to be taken lightly. They had learned that the truth could be a powerful force for change, but also a heavy burden to carry. And so, they approached the vine with reverence, understanding that the answers they received could shape their lives in ways they could not foresee.

In this way, the legend of the talking vine lived on, a story passed down through generations, a reminder that the truth, while sometimes difficult, was a path that could lead to understanding, growth, and ultimately, peace.

Cultural Significance and Facts about The Talking Vine

The Talking Vine is a lesser-known but culturally rich Italian folk tale that encapsulates many of the core elements of traditional storytelling from Italy. This tale, like many others from the region, serves as a vessel for conveying moral lessons, exploring human nature, and reflecting the intricate relationship between people and the supernatural. Though not as widely recognized as other Italian folk tales, The Talking Vine offers profound insights into the values and beliefs that have shaped Italian culture over centuries. Its significance lies not only in the narrative itself but also in the symbolic and allegorical meanings that can be drawn from the story.

The Role of Nature in Italian Folklore

In Italian folklore, nature often plays a central role, and The Talking Vine is a prime example of this tradition. The story centers around a vine, a plant that is deeply symbolic in Mediterranean culture. The vine is traditionally associated with life, growth, and fertility, particularly in a region where viticulture (the cultivation of grapes for wine) is an integral part of the economy and social life. In this tale, however, the vine transcends its agricultural significance to become a mystical entity capable of revealing hidden truths and shaping the destinies of those who seek its counsel.

The talking vine embodies the idea that nature is not just a passive backdrop to human activity but an active participant in the world, capable of influencing human lives in mysterious ways. This reflects a broader theme in Italian folklore, where natural elements *such as trees, rivers, and mountains are often imbued with spirits or magical properties. These stories convey the belief that the natural world is interconnected with the human world, and that there are forces at work that are beyond human understanding. The vine's ability to speak and reveal truths is a metaphor for the idea that nature itself holds wisdom and knowledge that humans can access, but only at a cost.*

Truth and Consequences: A Moral Exploration

At its core, The Talking Vine is a story about truth and the consequences of seeking it. The vine's revelations are a double-edged sword, offering clarity but also bringing pain and disruption to the lives of those who ask for its guidance. This theme is a common motif in folklore and literature, where the pursuit of knowledge often leads to unforeseen consequences. In this tale, the vine acts as a neutral entity, neither benevolent nor malevolent, simply revealing what is hidden. The real test lies in how the characters handle the truths they uncover.

This moral complexity reflects the Italian cultural understanding of truth as something that is not always straightforward or easy to accept. In a society where family, honor, and reputation are highly valued, the exposure of secrets can be particularly damaging. The story suggests that while truth is important, it must be approached with caution and wisdom. This is a lesson that resonates with the values of discretion and prudence, which are often emphasized in Italian culture. The tale warns against the dangers of delving too deeply into matters that might be best left alone, highlighting the fine balance between curiosity and wisdom.

The Symbolism of the Vine

The vine itself is a potent symbol in the story, representing a connection between the earthly and the divine, the known and the unknown. In Mediterranean cultures, the vine is traditionally associated with Dionysus, the Greek god of wine, who represents both the pleasures and dangers of intoxication, excess, and the ecstatic release from the ordinary world. In The Talking Vine, however, the vine's role is more subdued and contemplative. It is not a source of wild revelry but of quiet, introspective truth. This aligns the vine more with the concept of wisdom—ancient, rooted, and sometimes difficult to bear.

The vine's deep roots symbolize the hidden depths of the human soul, where secrets and truths are buried. The act of approaching the vine, asking it questions, and listening to its whispering leaves is a metaphor for the process of self-examination and the search for inner truth. The story encourages introspection and suggests that true wisdom comes from understanding oneself and one's place in the world. However, it also cautions that this understanding comes with responsibility, as the truths revealed can be unsettling and disruptive.

The fact that the vine grows on an ancient stone wall at the edge of the village further enhances its symbolic significance. The wall represents the boundary between the known world of the village and the unknown world beyond—both literally and figuratively. The vine, straddling this boundary, is a bridge between these two worlds, suggesting that the truths it reveals are not entirely of this world. This duality speaks to the idea that the knowledge gained from the vine is both a gift and a burden, something that can enlighten but also unsettle the foundations of everyday life.

The Stranger as a Catalyst for Change

The arrival of the stranger in the story serves as a narrative catalyst, a common trope in folk tales where an outsider brings about change or disruption to a community. In The Talking Vine, the stranger's curiosity and persistence set off a chain of events that lead to the uncovering of hidden truths and the subsequent turmoil in the village. The stranger's role is essential, as it is through his interactions with the vine that the story's themes are fully explored.

The stranger represents the human desire for knowledge and understanding, a desire that drives individuals to seek out answers, even at great personal risk. His journey to the village and his encounter with the vine symbolize the quest for truth that is inherent in the human condition. However, the stranger also embodies the idea that seeking truth is not a neutral act; it has consequences not just for the seeker but for those around them. His interactions with the villagers and the vine illustrate how the pursuit of knowledge can disrupt established social orders and bring hidden tensions to the surface.

In many ways, the stranger's journey mirrors that of the reader or listener of the tale, who is also seeking understanding through the story. The tale invites the audience to consider their own relationship with truth and knowledge, and to reflect on the potential consequences of their own quests for understanding. The stranger's ultimate realization—that the truth is a burden as much as it is a revelation—serves as a cautionary note to all who would seek to uncover what is hidden.

The Impact on the Village

The village in The Talking Vine is a microcosm of a traditional Italian community, where close-knit relationships and social harmony are highly valued. The vine's revelations, which expose secrets and hidden resentments, threaten the stability of this community. This aspect of the story highlights the delicate balance that exists within small communities, where everyone's actions and secrets are interconnected.

The story suggests that while truth is valuable, it can also be dangerous if not handled with care. The villagers' initial reactions to the vine's revelations—anger, betrayal, and suspicion—are natural responses to having their private lives exposed. However, the story also shows that truth, when approached with humility and understanding, can lead to healing and reconciliation. The stranger's efforts to help the villagers come to terms with the vine's revelations demonstrate the potential for growth and renewal, even in the face of difficult truths.

This theme of community and reconciliation is a reflection of the Italian cultural emphasis on family and social bonds. In Italy, the concept of "la famiglia" extends beyond the immediate family to include the broader community, and maintaining harmony within this extended family is a key cultural value. The story underscores the importance of communication, forgiveness, and understanding in preserving these bonds, even when they are tested by difficult truths.

The Vine as a Moral Arbiter

In some interpretations, the vine can be seen as a moral arbiter, revealing truths that are meant to guide individuals toward better behavior and greater self-awareness. The vine's ability to expose secrets serves as a reminder that actions have consequences and that nothing can remain hidden forever. This moral dimension of the story aligns with the broader tradition of folk tales serving as vehicles for imparting ethical lessons.

However, the story also complicates this interpretation by showing that the truth is not always a straightforward path to righteousness. The vine's revelations are not always welcome, and they often bring pain before they bring healing. This reflects the complexity of moral decision-making in real life, where the right course of action is not always clear, and where the consequences of one's choices can be difficult to predict.

The vine's role as a moral arbiter is therefore ambiguous—it reveals the truth, but it does not dictate how that truth should be handled. The responsibility for interpreting and acting on the vine's revelations falls to the individuals who seek its counsel. This places the burden of moral judgment squarely on the shoulders of the characters, and by extension, on the audience. The story encourages readers and listeners to consider their own moral choices and the potential consequences of seeking or revealing the truth.

The Legacy of The Talking Vine in Italian Culture

While The Talking Vine may not be as widely known as other Italian folk tales, it remains an important part of the country's rich storytelling tradition. The tale is a testament to the enduring power of folklore to explore complex themes such as truth, morality, and the human condition. It also reflects the deep cultural connection between the people of Italy and the natural world, where elements of nature are often seen as imbued with wisdom and spiritual *significance.*

In modern times, the story of The Talking Vine continues to resonate with audiences who are drawn to its exploration of truth and consequence. The tale has been adapted into various forms, including literature, theater, and even film, each interpretation bringing new layers of meaning to the story. Its themes of self-examination, the burden of knowledge, and the importance of community remain relevant in a world where the pursuit of truth is often fraught with uncertainty.

The vine itself, as a symbol of both nature and knowledge, has taken on a life of its own in Italian culture. It represents the idea that wisdom is something that grows slowly, rooted deeply in the earth, and that it must be approached with respect and caution. The vine's dual nature—offering both guidance and challenge—mirrors the complexities of life, where every choice carries weight and every truth has its price.

Conclusion

The Talking Vine is a rich and nmulti-layered folk tale that offers profound insights into the human experience. Through its exploration of truth, consequence, and the power of nature, the story invites readers to reflect on their own lives and the choices they make. It serves as a reminder that the pursuit of knowledge is a journey fraught with challenges, but also one that can lead to greater understanding and growth.

In the end, The Talking Vine is more than just a story—it is a mirror, reflecting the hopes, fears, and desires of those who listen to it. It reminds us that the truth, while sometimes difficult, is an essential part of our journey through life, and that it is only through facing that truth that we can truly find peace and understanding.

As the vine whispers its secrets to those who dare to listen, it continues to offer wisdom and guidance, helping each new generation navigate the complexities of the world around them.

The Tale of the Laughing Apple

In a small, sun-drenched village nestled in the rolling hills of Italy, there lived a poor but kind-hearted farmer named Giuseppe. Giuseppe was known throughout the village for his generosity and his willingness to help others, even though he had little to give. He lived alone in a modest cottage on the edge of the village, tending to a small plot of land that had been in his family for generations. The soil was rocky and difficult to cultivate, but Giuseppe worked tirelessly, eking out a humble living by growing vegetables and a few fruit trees.

One summer, as Giuseppe was tending to his garden, he noticed something strange happening in a far corner of his land. There, among the wildflowers and tall grasses, stood an apple tree that he had never seen before. The tree was unlike any other in his orchard. Its bark was smooth and silvery, and its branches were laden with the most unusual apples—large, golden, and glowing softly in the afternoon sunlight.

Curious, Giuseppe approached the tree and plucked one of the apples from its branch. It felt warm in his hand, and as he examined it more closely, he noticed something extraordinary—the apple seemed to be quivering slightly, as if it were alive. Before he could make sense of what he was seeing, the apple emitted a soft, melodic sound—a sound that grew louder until Giuseppe realized that the apple was laughing!

Startled, Giuseppe nearly dropped the apple, but his curiosity got the better of him. He brought the apple close to his ear and listened as it continued to laugh, its sound infectious and full of joy. Unable to resist, Giuseppe took a bite of the apple. The moment the sweet, juicy fruit touched his lips, he felt a wave of happiness wash over him. It was as if all his worries and cares melted away, replaced by a deep, bubbling joy that made him want to laugh out loud.

Giuseppe marveled at the apple's effect on him. He had never felt such pure happiness in his life, and he knew that the apple was no ordinary fruit. As he finished eating, the laughter in the apple gradually faded, but the feeling of joy lingered, filling him with a sense of contentment and peace.

In the days that followed, Giuseppe couldn't stop thinking about the laughing apple. He returned to the tree often, plucking a few more apples and sharing them with his neighbors. Each time someone ate one of the apples, they too were overcome with happiness, their laughter echoing through the village. Word quickly spread about the miraculous tree on Giuseppe's land, and soon people from all over the village were coming to see it for themselves.

Giuseppe, ever the generous soul, shared the apples freely with anyone who needed a bit of joy in their lives. He gave them to the children who had lost their parents, to the elderly who were lonely, and to the sick who were in pain. The apples brought light and laughter to the village, and soon it became known as the happiest place in the region.

The tree continued to produce its magical fruit, and Giuseppe noticed that it never seemed to run out of apples. No matter how many he picked, new ones would appear the next day, ready to bring joy to whoever ate them. The villagers began to call the tree "L'Albero delle Risate," the Laughing Tree, and they treated it with great reverence, knowing that it was a gift that should be cherished and respected.

But while the village thrived in its newfound happiness, the story of the laughing apple soon spread beyond its borders. Travelers passing through the village told tales of the magical tree to everyone they met, and before long, the legend of the laughing apple reached the ears of a powerful and greedy king who ruled over the land.

The king, whose name was Vittorio, was a man who desired wealth and power above all else. He lived in a grand palace filled with treasures from across the world, but despite his riches, he was a deeply unhappy man. Nothing seemed to bring him joy, and he was constantly searching for something—anything—that could fill the emptiness in his heart.

When King Vittorio heard about the laughing apple, he was immediately intrigued. He had never heard of a fruit that could bring such happiness, and he decided that he must have it for himself. If the apple could make him laugh, perhaps it could also fill the void that nothing else had been able to satisfy.

Without delay, King Vittorio summoned his most trusted advisor, a cunning and ambitious man named Ludovico. "Ludovico," the king said, "I have heard of a miraculous apple that brings joy to all who eat it. It is said to grow in a small village not far from here. I want you to go to this village and bring me the laughing apple. Do whatever it takes to acquire it."

Ludovico, always eager to please the king, set off

immediately for the village. He traveled for several days, through forests and over hills, until he finally reached Giuseppe's village. When he arrived, he saw the villagers smiling and laughing, their faces bright with joy. It was clear that the tales of the laughing apple were true.

Ludovico wasted no time in seeking out Giuseppe. He found the farmer tending to his garden, a smile on his face as he worked. "You must be Giuseppe," Ludovico said, approaching him with a calculating look in his eyes. "I have heard of your miraculous tree and the apples it bears. I have come on behalf of King Vittorio to purchase these apples from you. Name your price, and the king will pay it."

Giuseppe, who had always shared the apples freely with his neighbors, was taken aback by the request. He had never considered selling the apples, and the idea of exchanging such a precious gift for money troubled him. "The apples are not for sale," Giuseppe replied gently. "They are meant to bring joy to those who need it. I cannot put a price on happiness."

Ludovico was not used to being refused, and his face darkened with anger. "The king is not accustomed to hearing no," he said, his voice cold. "You would be wise to reconsider. The king is willing to pay handsomely for these apples, and you could live in comfort for the rest of your days. Surely that is worth more than a few apples?"

But Giuseppe was firm. "These apples are a gift," he said. "They are not mine to sell. If the king wishes to have one, he is welcome to come and share in the joy, just as everyone else in the village has done. But I will not sell them."

Ludovico left Giuseppe with a promise to return, his mind already scheming a way to get the apples by any means necessary. The kindness and generosity of the farmer had put him at odds with the greed of the king, and the tale of the laughing apple was about to take a dark turn.

After his encounter with Giuseppe, Ludovico returned to the king's palace, his mind churning with thoughts of how to fulfill his mission. King Vittorio was not a man to be denied what he wanted, and Ludovico knew that failure was not an option. As he rode through the countryside, he considered various schemes to obtain the laughing apples, but each one seemed riskier than the last. By the time he arrived at the palace, Ludovico had devised a plan that he was confident would succeed.

King Vittorio was waiting impatiently in the grand hall, his eyes narrowing as Ludovico approached. "Well?" the king demanded. "Did you bring me the laughing apple?"

Ludovico bowed deeply, masking his frustration with a polished smile. "Your Majesty, I regret to inform you that the farmer, Giuseppe, refused to sell the apples. He insists that they are a gift meant to bring joy and cannot be sold for money. However, I have a plan that will ensure the apples are yours."

The king's expression darkened at the mention of Giuseppe's refusal, but he motioned for Ludovico to continue. "Go on," he said curtly.

"Your Majesty," Ludovico began, "the farmer may refuse to sell the apples, but he is a simple man who values his village and his neighbors. We can use this to our advantage. If we were to apply pressure—perhaps by threatening the village with higher taxes or by taking away some of their land—I believe Giuseppe would relent. He will have no choice but to give you the apples in exchange for the safety and well-being of his fellow villagers."

King Vittorio considered this for a moment, his gaze turning cold and calculating. The idea of forcing Giuseppe's hand appealed to his sense of power and control. "Very well," the king said. "Do what you must to bring me the laughing apple. But be sure that the villagers understand the consequences of defying their king."

With the king's approval, Ludovico set his plan into motion. He returned to the village with a small contingent of soldiers, their presence an ominous reminder of the king's authority. The villagers, who had been enjoying the peace and happiness brought by the laughing apples, were unnerved by the sudden appearance of armed men in their midst. Whispers of fear spread quickly, and it wasn't long before Ludovico sought out Giuseppe once more.

This time, Ludovico was not alone. He arrived at Giuseppe's cottage flanked by soldiers, their faces stern and uncompromising. Giuseppe, who had been tending to the Laughing Tree, looked up in surprise as Ludovico approached.

"Giuseppe," Ludovico began, his tone far less friendly than before, "the king has made his wishes clear. He desires the laughing apples, and he will have them, one way or another. If you continue to refuse, the king will impose heavy taxes on the village, and your neighbors will suffer. If you care for them as much as you claim, you will give the apples to the king."

Giuseppe's heart sank at Ludovico's words. He had always believed in sharing the joy of the laughing apples freely, never imagining that his refusal to sell them could bring harm to his village. The thought of his neighbors being punished because of him was unbearable, and he found himself torn between his principles and his responsibility to those he cared about.

"Please," Giuseppe said, his voice filled with concern, "there must be another way. I cannot sell the apples, but I will gladly give one to the king if it will prevent harm from coming to the village. Let him come and take part in the joy that these apples bring, just as the villagers have."

Ludovico shook his head, his eyes hard. "The king is not interested in sharing the apples with others. He wants them for himself, and he will not accept anything less than complete ownership. If you will not sell them, then the village will pay the price."

Giuseppe looked around at the soldiers, their expressions unyielding, and he felt a wave of despair. He could not bear the thought of his neighbors suffering because of his actions, yet he knew that the apples were not meant to be hoarded by one man, no matter how powerful. The laughter and joy they brought were meant to be shared, not locked away in a king's palace.

After a long moment of silence, Giuseppe spoke again, his voice heavy with resignation. "If it will save the village, then I will give the apples to the king. But know this—by taking these apples for himself, the king is turning away from the true joy they bring. The laughter in these apples comes from sharing and bringing happiness to others, not from hoarding them out of greed."

Ludovico smirked, unmoved by Giuseppe's words. "The king will decide for himself what brings him joy," he replied coldly. "Prepare the apples. We will return to the palace at once."

Giuseppe, heartbroken but resolved, gathered a small basket of the laughing apples. He gently placed each one in the basket, feeling the warmth of the fruit and hearing the soft, joyful laughter that emanated from within. As he handed the basket to Ludovico, he felt as though he were saying goodbye to something precious, something that had brought so much light into his life and the lives of those around him.

Ludovico and the soldiers left the village with the basket of laughing apples, leaving behind a sense of unease and sadness. The villagers, who had seen the exchange from a distance, began to worry about what would happen next. They feared that without the laughing apples, the joy that had filled their village would fade, and they would return to the hardships and struggles of their previous lives.

As Ludovico returned to the palace, he couldn't help but feel a sense of triumph. He had accomplished his mission, and soon the king would have the laughing apples he so desired. But as he neared the palace, he began to wonder if Giuseppe's warning might hold some truth. The apples were meant to bring joy to many, not just one. What would happen if that joy were confined to the cold, greedy hands of a king who cared only for himself?

King Vittorio was waiting eagerly in the grand hall when Ludovico arrived. The moment he saw the basket of golden apples, his eyes lit up with anticipation. "At last!" the king exclaimed, reaching for one of the apples. "The source of happiness I have longed for!"

But as the king picked up the first apple, something unexpected happened. The apple, which had been warm and full of laughter in Giuseppe's hands, grew cold and silent in the king's grasp. The once joyful laughter that had echoed from within the apple faded, leaving only an eerie silence.

Puzzled, the king looked at Ludovico. "What is this?" he demanded. "Why is the apple no longer laughing?"

Ludovico, equally confused, could offer no explanation. "Your Majesty, I do not know. The apples laughed when they were in the village, but it seems that something has changed."

The king frowned, unwilling to believe that the apples could lose their magic. He took a bite of the apple, expecting to feel the joy that had been promised. But instead of the wave of happiness that Giuseppe had described, the king felt nothing. The fruit was sweet, but it brought him no joy, no laughter—only a hollow emptiness.

Frustrated and angry, King Vittorio threw the apple aside. "What trickery is this?" he shouted. "I was promised laughter and happiness, yet these apples are nothing but ordinary fruit!"

Ludovico, fearing the king's wrath, quickly tried to calm him. "Perhaps, Your Majesty, the magic of the apples lies in how they are shared. The farmer Giuseppe said that the laughter comes from bringing joy to others. Maybe if you were to share these apples with others, the laughter would return."

The king scowled, unwilling to accept that he would have to give up what he had so eagerly sought for himself. But as he looked at the basket of now-silent apples, he began to realize that there was some truth to Ludovico's words. The joy he had craved could not be taken by force; it could only be found through the act of giving.

Reluctantly, King Vittorio agreed to try sharing the apples. He invited the members of his court to a feast and instructed them to pass the apples among themselves. As each person took a bite, the laughter slowly returned, growing louder and more joyful with each apple that was shared. The once-silent apples were now filled with the same happiness that had filled Giuseppe's village, and the sound of laughter echoed through the palace halls.

King Vittorio watched as the joy spread among his courtiers, and for the first time in his life, he felt a flicker of true happiness. It was not the selfish, solitary joy he had imagined, but a shared experience, something that grew and multiplied as it was passed from person to person.

Realizing the lesson that Giuseppe had tried to impart, the

king sent a message to the village, apologizing for his greed and inviting Giuseppe to the palace. When Giuseppe arrived, King Vittorio thanked him for the apples and for teaching him the true meaning of happiness. From that day forward, the king made sure that the laughter of the apples was shared with everyone in the kingdom, spreading joy far and wide.

And so, the tale of the laughing apple became a legend, a story passed down through generations as a reminder that true happiness is not something that can be hoarded or taken by force. It is something that grows when shared, something that brings light and laughter to all who partake in it.

Cultural Significance and Facts about The Tale of the Laughing Apple

The Tale of the Laughing Apple is an Italian folk tale that, while perhaps lesser-known in comparison to some of the more famous stories in the Italian folklore canon, carries profound cultural significance. It is a tale that explores universal themes of generosity, greed, and the true nature of happiness—concepts that resonate deeply within Italian culture and, more broadly, within the human experience. The story of the laughing apple is not just about a magical fruit; it is a moral parable that offers insights into the values, traditions, and beliefs that have shaped Italian society over centuries.

The Role of Folklore in Italian Culture

Italian folklore is a rich tapestry woven from the country's diverse regional traditions, historical influences, and deep-rooted superstitions. Folk tales like *The Tale of the Laughing Apple* are essential components of this cultural heritage, serving as vehicles for transmitting moral lessons, cultural values, and collective wisdom from one generation to the next. These stories were often told in the context of family gatherings, village festivals, or around the hearth, where they played a crucial role in educating children and reinforcing community bonds.

The Tale of the Laughing Apple fits neatly into this tradition. Its narrative structure, with a clear moral lesson, is typical of Italian folk tales, which often feature simple yet profound stories that reflect the everyday lives and struggles of ordinary people. The tale's emphasis on generosity and the dangers of greed speaks to the values that have long been cherished in Italian culture, where family, community, and social harmony are paramount.

The Apple as a Symbol in Italian Culture

Apples hold significant symbolic meaning in many cultures, and Italy is no exception. In Italian folklore, the apple is often associated with knowledge, temptation, and the duality of good and evil. This symbolism is rooted in both Christian and pre-Christian traditions. For instance, the biblical story of Adam and Eve, where the apple is the forbidden fruit, has influenced many cultural interpretations of the fruit as a symbol of temptation and the consequences of desire.

However, in *The Tale of the Laughing Apple*, the apple takes on a different, more positive connotation. It becomes a symbol of joy, happiness, and the importance of sharing these emotions with others. The laughter emanating from the apple represents the infectious nature of joy—how happiness, when shared, can multiply and spread throughout a community. This shift in *symbolism from temptation to joy reflects the story's moral focus on the virtues of generosity and selflessness.*

In Italy, where the sharing of food is a central part of social life, the laughing apple can also be seen as a metaphor for the communal aspect of happiness. Just as food is shared among family and friends during meals, so too should happiness be shared to strengthen social bonds and bring people together. The story underscores the belief that true contentment comes not from hoarding wealth or pleasures for oneself, but from spreading joy and goodwill within the community.

The Moral of the Story: Generosity versus Greed

At the heart of The Tale of the Laughing Apple is a moral lesson about the dangers of greed and the virtues of generosity. The story contrasts the selfless character of Giuseppe, who freely shares the laughing apples with his fellow villagers, with the greedy King Vittorio, who seeks to possess the apples for himself. This dichotomy serves to highlight the destructive nature of greed and the ways in which it can blind individuals to the true sources of happiness.

Giuseppe's character embodies the ideal of la generosità, a deeply rooted cultural value in Italy. Generosity is not just seen as an individual virtue but as a social responsibility. In Italian culture, there is a strong emphasis on helping others, whether through hospitality, sharing food, or offering support in times of need. This value is often expressed in the concept of fare una buona figura, which means making a good impression, not through wealth or status, but through kindness, generosity, and consideration for others.

In contrast, King Vittorio represents the dangers of unchecked ambition and the false belief that happiness can be bought or possessed. His initial failure to find joy in the apples, despite having them all to himself, illustrates the emptiness of material wealth when it is not accompanied by meaningful connections with others. The king's eventual realization that the apples' laughter returns only when shared is a powerful reminder that true happiness is inherently social—it is found in relationships, community, and the act of giving.

This moral lesson is particularly resonant in Italian culture, where the well-being of the community often takes precedence over individual desires. The story reinforces the idea that wealth and power are not the ultimate sources of happiness; instead, fulfillment comes from contributing to the happiness of others. This message aligns with the broader Italian cultural emphasis on la famiglia (the family) and la comunità (the community) as the cornerstones of social life.

The Village as a Reflection of Italian Society

The village setting of The Tale of the Laughing Apple is a microcosm of traditional Italian society, where the community plays a central role in the lives of individuals. Villages in Italy have historically been close-knit communities where everyone knows each other, and social cohesion is maintained through shared customs, festivals, and mutual support. In such settings, the actions of one person can have significant ripple effects throughout the community, as seen in the story when Giuseppe's generosity brings joy to the entire village.

The villagers' initial reaction to the laughing apples—coming together to share in the happiness they bring—is indicative of the communal spirit that characterizes rural Italian life. In these communities, the success and well-being of one person are often seen as tied to the success and well-being of the whole village. This collective mentality is reflected in the story's emphasis on sharing the apples, which ensures that the joy they bring is experienced by everyone, not just a select few.

The disruption caused by Ludovico and the king's soldiers also serves as a commentary on the tension between the simple, harmonious life of the village and the often harsh, exploitative nature of external authority. In many Italian folk tales, kings and rulers are portrayed as distant, sometimes oppressive figures whose actions can disrupt the peace of rural life. This reflects historical realities, where local communities often had to navigate the demands of powerful lords or external rulers while striving to maintain their own traditions and way of life.

In the story, the villagers' fear of the king's retribution and the potential loss of their happiness underscores the vulnerability of small communities to the whims of those in power. However, the resolution of the tale, where the king learns the value of generosity and the importance of sharing, restores the balance and reaffirms the strength of the village's communal bonds. This outcome reflects the ideal of giustizia, or justice, a key theme in many Italian folk tales, where good ultimately triumphs over evil, and harmony is restored.

The Laughing Apple as a Symbol of Joy and the Power of Laughter

The laughter of the apple in the story is not just a whimsical detail; it is central to the tale's message about the transformative power of joy and laughter. Laughter, in many cultures, is seen as a universal language that can bridge differences, heal wounds, and bring people together. In Italian culture, where expressive communication and emotional warmth are highly valued, laughter holds a special place as a sign of genuine happiness and a means of fostering social connections.

The laughing apple symbolizes the contagious nature of joy—how a single source of happiness, when shared, can multiply and spread throughout a community. This idea is reinforced by the way the apple's laughter fades when it is hoarded by the king and only returns when it is shared among his court. The story suggests that joy, like laughter, is meant to be shared, and that it thrives in an environment of openness and generosity.

The apple's laughter also serves as a metaphor for the simple pleasures in life—those moments of pure, unadulterated joy that cannot be bought or forced but must be experienced and shared naturally. This reflects a key aspect of the Italian concept of la dolce vita—the sweet life—where the emphasis is on savoring the simple joys of life, whether it's a good meal, a beautiful landscape, or the company of loved ones. The laughing apple, with its ability to bring spontaneous joy, embodies this appreciation for the small, everyday moments that make life rich and fulfilling.

The King's Transformation: A Lesson in Humility and Wisdom

King Vittorio's transformation from a greedy, unhappy ruler to someone who understands the value of generosity is a crucial element of the story. It illustrates the idea that wisdom often comes through experience and that even those who seem most set in their ways can change when confronted with the right lesson.

In Italian culture, rulers and authority figures in folklore are often depicted as needing to learn humility and compassion. This *reflects a historical reality where rulers were expected to be giusto (just) and benevolo (benevolent), acting in the best interests of their people rather than pursuing their own selfish desires. The king's journey in The Tale of the Laughing Apple is one of self-discovery, where he learns that true happiness cannot be commanded or bought but must be nurtured through acts of kindness and generosity.*

The story's resolution, where the king begins to share the apples and experiences genuine joy for the first time, is a powerful reminder of the transformative power of humility. By learning to give rather than take, the king not only finds the happiness he was searching for but also strengthens the bonds within his court and, by extension, his kingdom. This theme of personal growth through humility is common in Italian folklore, where characters often undergo moral and emotional development, leading to a more just and harmonious society.

The Legacy of The Tale of the Laughing Apple in Italian Culture

Although The Tale of the Laughing Apple may not be as widely recognized as other Italian folk tales, it holds an important place in the cultural tradition of storytelling that has been passed down through generations. The story's emphasis on community, generosity, and the simple joys of life resonates with core Italian values, making it a tale that continues to be relevant in modern times.

The story's themes have found expression in various forms of Italian art, literature, and even social practices. For example, the idea of sharing food and joy, central to the tale, is reflected in the Italian tradition of convivialità—the practice of eating and celebrating together as a way of strengthening social bonds. The story also serves as a reminder of the importance of resisting greed and materialism, values that are particularly relevant in a world where consumerism often threatens to overshadow more meaningful pursuits.

In contemporary Italy, where the preservation of cultural heritage is highly valued, stories like The Tale of the Laughing Apple are often revisited in schools, local festivals, and family gatherings. They serve as a connection to the past, offering timeless lessons that continue to shape the present and future. The laughing apple, with its magical ability to bring joy, remains a symbol of the enduring power of generosity and the belief that true happiness is found not in what we keep for ourselves but in what we give to others.

Conclusion

The Tale of the Laughing Apple is a rich and evocative folk tale that encapsulates key aspects of Italian cultural identity. Through its exploration of themes like generosity, greed, community, and the pursuit of happiness, the story offers a timeless lesson about the nature of true joy. It reminds us that happiness is not something to be hoarded or bought, but something that grows and multiplies when shared.

The laughing apple itself serves as a powerful symbol of this truth, representing the contagious nature of joy and the importance of maintaining a generous spirit. In a world where material wealth and power are often mistaken for true fulfillment, the tale offers a counter-narrative, one that emphasizes the value of simple pleasures, communal bonds, and the transformative power of giving.

As a part of Italy's rich tapestry of folklore, The Tale of the Laughing Apple continues to inspire and teach, ensuring that its lessons of kindness, humility, and shared happiness remain relevant for generations to come.

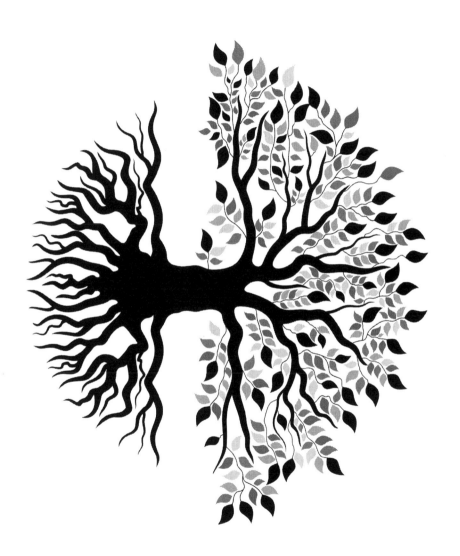

The Legend of the Tarantella

In the sun-soaked region of Puglia, nestled in the heel of Italy's boot, there lies a landscape of olive groves, vineyards, and ancient stone villages. This region, known for its rich cultural heritage and traditions, is also the birthplace of one of Italy's most famous folk dances—the tarantella. But the origins of this lively, rhythmic dance are steeped in legend and superstition, woven from the fears and beliefs of the people who lived in this land centuries ago.

Long ago, in the fields and forests of Southern Italy, there was a creature that inspired both terror and fascination among the villagers—the tarantula. This large, hairy spider was feared not only for its size but for the bite that it could inflict, a bite that was believed to carry a venom with strange and dangerous properties. According to local legend, the bite of the tarantula would send its victim into a state of hysteria, causing violent convulsions, delirium, and an uncontrollable urge to move. The afflicted person would fall into a deep, feverish state, their body wracked with pain and their mind consumed by strange visions.

This mysterious condition became known as "tarantism," and

it was believed that the only cure for this venom-induced madness was to engage in a frenzied, ecstatic dance. The dance, known as the tarantella, was said to drive the venom from the body through sweat and exhaustion, restoring the victim to health and sanity. The dance would continue until the afflicted person collapsed in exhaustion, their body purged of the spider's poison.

The story of the tarantella begins with a young woman named Alessandra, who lived in a small village on the outskirts of Puglia. Alessandra was known for her beauty and grace, and she often spent her days working in the fields, tending to the crops that sustained her family. One hot summer's day, as Alessandra was harvesting wheat under the blazing sun, she felt a sharp sting on her ankle. Looking down, she saw the unmistakable form of a tarantula scurrying away into the tall grass.

Panic seized Alessandra as the pain from the bite began to spread through her leg. She had heard the stories of what the tarantula's venom could do, how it could drive a person mad with its poison. Her heart raced, and she stumbled back toward the village, desperate to find help before the venom took hold.

By the time Alessandra reached the village square, the effects of the bite were already beginning to show. Her skin was pale, her eyes wide with fear, and her body trembled uncontrollably. The villagers gathered around her, their faces etched with concern as they realized what had happened. They knew that there was little time before the venom consumed her entirely.

An elderly woman, known in the village for her knowledge of herbs and remedies, stepped forward. "We must act quickly," she said, her voice firm. "The venom is spreading, but there is a way to save her."

The villagers listened intently as the woman explained the ritual that had been passed down through generations. They would need to play music—lively, fast-paced music that would compel Alessandra to dance. The rhythm of the music would guide her movements, helping her to expel the poison through sweat and exertion. The musicians in the village quickly gathered their instruments—tambourines, mandolins, and flutes—and began to play.

At first, Alessandra was too weak to move, her body heavy with the weight of the venom. But as the music swirled around her, something in the rhythm seemed to awaken a spark within her. Her feet began to twitch, then to shuffle, and soon she was moving in time with the beat. The villagers watched in awe as Alessandra, her movements becoming more vigorous with each passing moment, began to dance.

The dance was wild and unrestrained, her body twisting and turning with a desperate energy. She spun in circles, her arms flailing, her feet stamping the ground in a frantic rhythm. The music grew louder and faster, driving her on, and the villagers clapped and cheered, urging her to continue. Alessandra danced until her clothes were soaked with sweat, her hair clinging to her face, her breaths coming in ragged gasps.

Finally, after what seemed like hours, Alessandra collapsed to the ground, her body utterly spent. The music stopped, and the villagers rushed to her side, their hearts pounding with fear and hope. But as they bent over her, they saw that her breathing had steadied, and the wild look in her eyes had faded. The venom had been driven out, and Alessandra, though exhausted, was saved.

Word of Alessandra's miraculous recovery spread quickly

through the surrounding villages. The tale of how the tarantella had saved her from the deadly bite of the tarantula became the stuff of legend, and soon others began to turn to the dance as a cure for tarantism. Whenever someone was bitten by a tarantula, the villagers would gather, their instruments at the ready, and the afflicted person would dance the tarantella until the venom was expelled.

The tarantella dance became a powerful symbol of resistance against the forces of nature that threatened the lives of the villagers. It was a way of reclaiming control over one's body and mind, of fighting back against the madness that the tarantula's bite could bring. But more than that, it was a celebration of life, of the vitality and energy that coursed through the human spirit even in the face of danger.

As the years passed, the tarantella evolved from a ritualistic dance into a beloved folk tradition. No longer just a cure for tarantism, it became a communal dance performed at festivals, weddings, and other celebrations. The lively rhythm and intricate steps of the tarantella captured the joy and passion of the Italian people, and it soon spread beyond Puglia, becoming popular throughout Southern Italy and beyond.

The music of the tarantella, with its rapid tempo and lively melodies, was passed down through generations, each region adding its own variations and flourishes to the dance. The tambourine, with its sharp, percussive sound, became the iconic instrument of the tarantella, accompanied by the mandolin, accordion, and other traditional instruments. The dance itself was characterized by quick, light steps, often performed in a circle or as a couple's dance, with partners exchanging playful glances and gestures as they moved in time with the music.

In some villages, the tarantella retained its connection to the legend of the tarantula, and it was still performed as part of rituals to ward off the effects of tarantism. But in most places, it had become a symbol of celebration and joy, a way for communities to come together and express their shared love of life and tradition.

The legend of the tarantella is more than just a story about a dance; it is a reflection of the resilience and creativity of the Italian people. Faced with the fear of the unknown, they turned to music and dance as a way of healing and finding joy in the midst of adversity. The tarantella, with its infectious energy and vibrant rhythms, is a testament to the enduring power of culture to bring people together, to heal, and to celebrate the beauty of life.

Cultural Significance and Facts about The Legend of the Tarantella

The Legend of the Tarantella is a rich and multifaceted tale that is deeply ingrained in the cultural fabric of Southern Italy, particularly in the regions of Puglia, Calabria, and Campania. This story is not merely about a dance; it is a reflection of the historical, social, and psychological dimensions of life in these regions. The tarantella, with its fast-paced rhythms and lively movements, has transcended its origins as a folk remedy for tarantism to become a symbol of Italian cultural identity and a celebration of life. The legend associated with the tarantella offers profound insights into how folklore, music, and dance can serve as tools for healing, community cohesion, and the expression of collective identity.

The Historical Context of Tarantism and the Tarantella

The origins of the tarantella are closely linked to the phenomenon of tarantism, a psychosomatic condition believed to be caused by the bite of the tarantula spider, particularly the Lycosa tarantula, which is native to the Mediterranean region. The condition was first documented in the 15th century and continued to be a significant cultural and medical concern in Southern Italy well into the 18th and 19th centuries.

Tarantism was characterized by symptoms such as severe pain, delirium, convulsions, and a hysterical need to move. Those afflicted were often said to experience uncontrollable urges to dance, which were believed to be the body's natural response to expel the venom. In the absence of modern medical treatments, the people of Southern Italy turned to music and dance as a form of therapeutic intervention.

The tarantella dance, which emerged as a ritualistic response to tarantism, was believed to have the power to cure the afflicted by inducing a state of ecstasy and exhaustion. The frantic, rhythmic movements of the dance were thought to help expel the venom from the body through sweat, while the repetitive, hypnotic music provided a psychological release from the grip of the venom-induced madness.

This practice was deeply rooted in the local belief systems and reflects the broader historical context of the time. In medieval and early modern Europe, where medical knowledge was limited, folk remedies and rituals played a crucial role in addressing physical and mental health issues. The tarantella, therefore, can be seen as a form of traditional medicine, one that combined physical movement with the power of music and community support to *heal both the body and the mind.*

The Symbolism of the Tarantella

The tarantella is imbued with rich symbolism that goes beyond its practical application as a cure for tarantism. At its core, the dance represents a struggle between life and death, order and chaos, reason and madness. The tarantula's bite, with its potentially deadly consequences, symbolizes the unpredictable dangers that life can bring, while the dance itself represents the human spirit's resilience and determination to overcome these challenges.

In this way, the tarantella embodies the concept of trionfo della vita—the triumph of life over death. The dance is a celebration of vitality, of the body's ability to move and express itself even in the face of illness or despair. It is an assertion of life's energy, of the joy that can be found even in the midst of suffering. This theme resonates deeply in Italian culture, where celebrations of life, often in the face of hardship, are a central part of the cultural identity.

The music of the tarantella, with its rapid tempo and driving rhythms, also carries symbolic weight. The fast, repetitive patterns of the music mirror the heartbeat, the pulse of life itself. The rhythm is both relentless and liberating, pushing the dancer to the edge of physical and mental endurance while also providing a sense of release and catharsis. This duality—of pressure and release, of tension and freedom—is a key element of the tarantella's power and appeal.

The circular nature of the dance, often performed in a ring or with dancers moving in a circular pattern, is another important symbolic element. Circles are powerful symbols in many cultures, representing unity, continuity, and the cycles of life. In the context of the tarantella, the circle may represent the cyclical nature of life and death, as well as the idea of communal support and solidarity. The dance is not just an individual experience but a collective one, with the community coming together to help the afflicted person through their ordeal.

The Evolution of the Tarantella

Over time, the tarantella evolved from a specific ritual associated with the cure of tarantism into a broader cultural practice, one that is celebrated today as a symbol of Italian heritage. As the belief in tarantism waned with the advancement of medical science, the tarantella was gradually transformed into a popular folk dance, performed at festivals, weddings, and other social gatherings.

This evolution reflects the adaptability of folk traditions and their ability to survive and thrive by taking on new meanings. While the original context of the tarantella as a cure for tarantism may have faded, the dance itself remained deeply embedded in the cultural consciousness of Southern Italy. Its lively rhythms, vibrant music, and energetic movements made it a natural fit for celebrations and social events, where it could bring people together in a shared experience of joy and community.

As the tarantella spread throughout Italy and beyond, different regions began to develop their own variations of the dance, each with its own unique style and musical accompaniment. In Naples, for example, the tarantella became associated with the city's rich musical tradition, and the dance was often performed with the accompaniment of mandolins, tambourines, and accordions. In Sicily, the tarantella took on a slightly different character, with influences from the island's diverse cultural history, including

Greek, Arab, and Spanish elements.

The tarantella's evolution from a healing ritual to a popular folk dance also highlights the broader cultural significance of dance in Italian society. Dance has long been a vital part of Italian life, serving as a means of expression, socialization, and cultural continuity. The tarantella, with its roots in both the sacred and the secular, embodies this dual role, connecting the spiritual and the communal in a way that is both deeply meaningful and profoundly enjoyable.

The Role of Women in the Tarantella

Women have played a central role in the history and practice of the tarantella, both as the primary subjects of the dance in its original context and as active participants in its evolution as a folk tradition. In the legend of the tarantella, it is often women who are depicted as being bitten by the tarantula and who must dance to cure themselves of the venom's effects. This focus on women reflects broader themes in Italian folklore, where women are frequently portrayed as both vulnerable to supernatural forces and as powerful figures capable of overcoming adversity.

The tarantella can be seen as a form of embodied resistance, where women, through the act of dancing, reclaim control over their bodies and their destinies. The dance is a way of asserting agency in the face of a condition that threatens to strip them of their autonomy. In this sense, the tarantella is not just a cure but a form of empowerment, a way for women to transform their vulnerability into strength.

This theme of empowerment is further reinforced by the communal nature of the dance. In many versions of the legend, the afflicted woman is surrounded by other women who play music, sing, and encourage her as she dances. This support network reflects the importance of female solidarity in Italian culture, where women often relied on each other for emotional and practical support in a society that was traditionally patriarchal.

As the tarantella evolved into a popular folk dance, women continued to play a prominent role as dancers, musicians, and keepers of the tradition. The dance provided a space for women to express themselves, to celebrate their bodies and their culture, and to participate in the social life of their communities. Even today, the tarantella remains a powerful symbol of female strength and resilience in Southern Italy, a reminder of the important role that women have played in preserving and transmitting cultural traditions.

The Cultural Legacy of the Tarantella

The tarantella's legacy is far-reaching, extending beyond its origins in Southern Italy to become a symbol of Italian culture recognized around the world. The dance has been featured in countless films, operas, and pieces of classical music, often serving as a shorthand for Italian identity and vibrancy. Composers such as Rossini, Chopin, and Berlioz have all written works inspired by the tarantella, incorporating its distinctive rhythms and energy into their compositions.

In popular culture, the tarantella is often associated with the festive spirit of Italy, evoking images of lively street festivals, vibrant costumes, and the joy of communal celebration. It has become a cultural ambassador for Italy, representing the country's rich heritage and the warmth and exuberance of its people. The tarantella's music and dance steps are taught in schools and performed at cultural events, ensuring that the tradition continues *to be passed down through generations.*

In Southern Italy, particularly in Puglia, the tarantella is celebrated as part of the region's cultural heritage. Festivals dedicated to the tarantella and the legend of the tarantula are held annually, attracting visitors from around the world who come to experience the dance in its original context. These festivals often feature performances by traditional musicians and dancers, workshops on the history and techniques of the tarantella, and opportunities for participants to join in the dance themselves.

The continued popularity of the tarantella is a testament to its enduring appeal and its ability to adapt to changing cultural contexts. While the original belief in tarantism may have faded, the tarantella has survived as a living tradition, one that continues to bring people together in a shared experience of music, movement, and joy. It is a reminder of the power of culture to heal, to connect, and to celebrate the beauty of life.

The Psychological and Social Dimensions of the Tarantella

The legend of the tarantella also offers insights into the psychological and social dimensions of illness and healing. Tarantism, as understood in the context of the legend, can be seen as a form of psychosomatic illness, where the symptoms are real but are deeply intertwined with the cultural beliefs and expectations of the community. The dance, with its intense physical exertion and rhythmic music, provided a way for individuals to express and release the psychological tension associated with the condition.

In this sense, the tarantella can be seen as an early form of dance therapy, where movement and music are used to achieve a therapeutic effect. The dance allowed individuals to channel their fear, anxiety, and physical discomfort into a structured activity that offered both physical and emotional release. The communal aspect of the dance, with the involvement of musicians, family members, and other community members, provided additional psychological support, reinforcing the idea that the afflicted person was not alone in their struggle.

The social dimension of the tarantella is also significant. In a close-knit rural community, where social harmony and cooperation were essential for survival, the dance served as a way of reinforcing social bonds and ensuring the well-being of the community as a whole. By coming together to perform the tarantella, the villagers demonstrated their commitment to each other and to the preservation of their cultural traditions. The dance was not just a cure for the individual; it was a ritual that reaffirmed the values of the community and the interconnectedness of its members.

The Tarantella in Modern Times

Today, the tarantella is celebrated not only in Italy but around the world as a symbol of Italian culture and heritage. It is performed at Italian cultural festivals, weddings, and other social events, where it continues to bring joy and a sense of connection to participants. In recent years, there has been a resurgence of interest in the tarantella, with musicians, dancers, and cultural historians working to preserve and revitalize the tradition.

In Puglia, the tarantella has become a focal point of cultural tourism, with visitors coming to the region to learn about the history of the dance and to experience it firsthand. Workshops, dance classes, and performances are offered by cultural *organizations and local communities, ensuring that the tradition remains vibrant and accessible to new generations.*

The tarantella has also found a place in contemporary dance and music, with artists experimenting with new interpretations and fusions of the traditional form. These modern adaptations often blend elements of the tarantella with other dance and music styles, creating innovative works that honor the past while engaging with the present. This ongoing evolution of the tarantella reflects its adaptability and its continued relevance in a changing world.

Conclusion

The Legend of the Tarantella is a powerful and enduring story that offers deep insights into the cultural, psychological, and social dimensions of life in Southern Italy. The tarantella, with its roots in the ancient ritual of curing tarantism, has evolved into a beloved folk tradition that continues to be celebrated and cherished today. It is a dance that embodies the resilience, vitality, and joy of the Italian people, and it serves as a reminder of the power of culture to heal, connect, and celebrate life.

Through its lively rhythms, symbolic movements, and communal spirit, the tarantella tells a story of triumph over adversity, of the strength that comes from community, and of the enduring appeal of music and dance as expressions of the human experience. As a cultural symbol, the tarantella is a testament to the rich heritage of Southern Italy and a celebration of the beauty and complexity of Italian identity.

In a world that often feels disconnected and fragmented, the tarantella offers a powerful reminder of the importance of tradition, community, and the simple joys of life. It is a dance that has the power to bring people together, to heal both body and soul, and to remind us all of the enduring power of culture to enrich our lives.

The Legend of the Olive Tree

In the sun-kissed lands of Southern Italy, where the rolling hills meet the azure waters of the Mediterranean, there stands an ancient tree that has been a witness to the passage of time, a symbol of peace and prosperity for countless generations. This is the olive tree, revered not only for its fruit but also for the deep roots it has planted in the culture and history of the region. Its twisted, gnarled trunk and silvery-green leaves tell the story of a land and its people, a story that has been passed down through the ages in the form of a legend—the Legend of the Olive Tree.

Long before the olive tree became a staple of Mediterranean life, its origins were shrouded in mystery and myth. The people of this land believed that the olive tree was not merely a plant but a divine gift, bestowed upon humanity by the gods themselves. The legend of the olive tree is a tale of creation, of the earth's bounty, and of the enduring connection between humans and nature.

The story begins in a time when the world was still young, and the gods walked among mortals, guiding them and shaping their destinies. The land that would one day become known as Italy was rich and fertile, but it was also wild and untamed, a place where nature's power was both revered and feared. The people who lived there were skilled farmers and shepherds, but they often struggled to tame the land and make it yield the food and resources they needed to survive.

One day, a great contest arose among the gods. They sought to prove who among them could create the most useful and precious gift for humanity. Each god, eager to demonstrate their power and wisdom, chose a different gift to present to the mortals. Some created rivers that would nourish the crops, others brought forth fruits and grains, and still others fashioned tools and weapons to aid in hunting and building.

But there were two gods whose rivalry was the fiercest—Athena, the goddess of wisdom and war, and Poseidon, the god of the sea. Both were determined to create a gift that would be remembered for all time, one that would not only benefit humanity but also ensure that their name would be honored and revered by future generations.

Poseidon, with his mighty trident, struck the earth and caused a great spring to burst forth. The waters surged from the ground, powerful and brimming with energy, creating a vast lake in the heart of the land. The people marveled at the sight, for the lake was a source of life, providing them with water to drink, to irrigate their fields, and to sustain their livestock.

But Athena was not to be outdone. She walked among the people, observing their needs and desires, and she saw that while Poseidon's gift of water was valuable, it was not enough. The people needed something that would nourish them, something that would bring peace and prosperity to their lives. With this in mind, Athena approached a barren hill, and with a gentle touch of her hand, she brought forth a tree—the first olive tree.

The tree was small at first, but its branches were strong, and its leaves shimmered in the sunlight like silver. As the people gathered around, they saw that the tree bore fruit—small, green olives that were unlike anything they had ever seen before. Curious, they tasted the fruit, and though it was bitter, they sensed its potential.

Athena then showed them how to press the olives to extract a golden oil, an oil that could be used for cooking, for healing wounds, and for lighting their homes. The people were amazed by the versatility of the olive tree and its fruit, and they immediately recognized the greatness of Athena's gift. The olive tree provided not only sustenance but also peace, for the oil it produced was used to anoint kings and priests, to seal treaties, and to light the sacred lamps in temples.

The people declared Athena the victor of the contest, and in honor of her gift, they planted olive trees across the land. The trees flourished in the Mediterranean climate, their roots digging deep into the rocky soil, and soon the land was covered with groves of olive trees, their branches heavy with fruit.

Poseidon, though disappointed by his defeat, accepted the judgment of the people and retreated to his watery domain. But the rivalry between the gods did not end in anger. Instead, it gave birth to a lasting bond between the earth and the sea, for the olive tree could only thrive when nourished by both the soil and the waters of the earth. This balance, this harmony between the elements, became a central theme in the legend of the olive tree, a symbol of the delicate relationship between humanity and nature.

As the years passed, the olive tree became a symbol of

peace and prosperity. Its branches were used as offerings to the gods, as symbols of victory in athletic competitions, and as tokens of reconciliation between warring factions. The olive tree's fruit, with its bitter taste, was a reminder of the struggles and hardships of life, but the golden oil it produced was a symbol of the rewards that come from perseverance and wisdom.

The legend of the olive tree spread far and wide, and soon it was told not only in Italy but throughout the Mediterranean. Each region added its own variations to the tale, but the central message remained the same—the olive tree was a gift from the gods, a reminder of the importance of balance, harmony, and the enduring connection between the earth and its people.

Today, the olive tree continues to hold a special place in the hearts of the people of Italy. It is more than just a source of food and oil; it is a symbol of the land itself, of the resilience and strength of those who have cultivated it for centuries. The olive tree's twisted trunk and gnarled branches tell the story of a land that has seen wars and peace, hardship and prosperity, and yet has endured through it all.

In every village and town across Southern Italy, you will find olive trees standing as silent witnesses to the passage of time. Their roots dig deep into the earth, their branches stretch toward the sky, and their fruit continues to nourish both body and soul. The legend of the olive tree lives on in the stories told by the elders, in the rituals and traditions passed down through generations, and in the simple act of breaking bread dipped in olive oil, a tradition that connects the present to the distant past.

And so, the legend of the olive tree remains a vital part of Italy's cultural heritage, a reminder of the timeless values of peace, wisdom, and harmony with nature. It is a story that continues to inspire, to teach, and to bring people together, just as the olive tree itself has done for centuries.

Cultural Significance and Facts about The Legend of the Olive Tree

The Legend of the Olive Tree is a deeply rooted tale within the cultural heritage of Italy and the broader Mediterranean region. The olive tree, Olea europaea, is not just a plant but a symbol of life, endurance, and prosperity. It represents the intertwining of nature and human existence, embodying the values of peace, wisdom, and resilience. This legend, which traces the mythical origins of the olive tree to the hands of the gods, serves as a cultural touchstone that has shaped the agricultural practices, rituals, and collective identity of the people who have lived in the Mediterranean basin for millennia.

The Olive Tree in Mediterranean Culture and History

The olive tree is one of the oldest cultivated plants in the world, with its domestication dating back over 6,000 years in the Eastern Mediterranean. Archaeological evidence suggests that olive cultivation began in the region that is now modern-day Turkey, Syria, and Israel, before spreading westward to Greece, Italy, and Spain. The tree's long lifespan—often exceeding several centuries—and its ability to thrive in the arid, rocky soils of the Mediterranean climate have made it an enduring symbol of life and continuity in a region that has seen the rise and fall of countless civilizations.

In Mediterranean culture, the olive tree has always been more than just a source of food. It is a symbol of the deep connection between the land and its people, a connection that is reflected in the myths and legends surrounding the tree. The olive tree's resilience, its ability to survive drought, poor soil, and harsh conditions, has made it a metaphor for human endurance and the perseverance of communities that have faced adversity throughout history.

The legend that ties the olive tree to the goddess Athena is particularly significant. In ancient Greek mythology, Athena, the goddess of wisdom and war, competed with Poseidon, the god of the sea, to determine who would be the patron deity of the city of Athens. Poseidon struck the ground with his trident, creating a saltwater spring, a symbol of his power over the seas. Athena, in contrast, struck the ground with her spear and produced an olive tree. The olive tree, with its ability to provide food, oil, and wood, was seen as the more valuable gift, and Athena was chosen as the city's patron.

This myth underscores the olive tree's association with wisdom, peace, and prosperity. The tree's fruit, the olive, is a staple of the Mediterranean diet, and the oil extracted from it has been used for cooking, medicine, and religious rituals for thousands of years. The olive tree thus became a symbol of Athena's wisdom and the idea that true power lies not in brute force but in the ability to provide for the needs of the community.

The Olive Tree as a Symbol of Peace

One of the most enduring symbols associated with the olive tree is that of peace. The olive branch has long been recognized as a symbol of peace and reconciliation. This association can be traced back to ancient Greece and Rome, where the olive branch was used as a token of peace, often carried by messengers and diplomats to signify their peaceful intentions. The symbol was later adopted by early Christians and became associated with the story of Noah's Ark, where a dove returned to the ark with an olive branch in its beak, signaling the end of the flood and the restoration of peace between God and humanity.

The olive branch's symbolism as a peace offering is also linked to the tree's long life and its ability to regenerate even after being cut down. This regenerative quality of the olive tree serves as a metaphor for the resilience of peace, suggesting that even in times of conflict and destruction, peace can be restored and life can begin anew.

In Italy, the olive tree has been a symbol of peace in both historical and contemporary contexts. During the Italian Renaissance, olive branches were often depicted in art as symbols of peace and prosperity. The tree itself was seen as a unifying symbol for the various regions of Italy, which were often embroiled in political and territorial disputes. The olive tree's ability to thrive in different parts of the country, from the rocky hills of Tuscany to the sun-drenched plains of Puglia, made it a symbol of the shared cultural and agricultural heritage of the Italian people.

Today, the olive branch continues to be a powerful symbol of peace in international diplomacy. The emblem of the United Nations features a world map surrounded by olive branches, representing the organization's commitment to promoting peace and cooperation among nations. This modern usage of the olive branch as a symbol of peace reflects the deep cultural significance that the tree has held for thousands of years.

The Olive Tree and the Mediterranean Diet

The olive tree is at the heart of the Mediterranean diet, which is widely regarded as one of the healthiest in the world. Olive oil, the primary product of the olive tree, is a staple of this diet, used in everything from cooking and salad dressings to marinades and sauces. The health benefits of olive oil have been well documented, with studies showing that it can help reduce the risk of heart disease, lower cholesterol levels, and provide antioxidants that protect against chronic diseases.

The legend of the olive tree ties into the idea of the Mediterranean diet as a gift from the gods—a way of life that is not only healthy but also deeply connected to the land and its traditions. In Italy, olive oil is often referred to as "liquid gold," a reflection of its value and importance in daily life. The process of producing olive oil, from harvesting the olives to pressing them into oil, is steeped in tradition and is often a communal activity that brings families and communities together.

In many parts of Italy, the olive harvest is a time of celebration, with festivals and feasts marking the end of the harvest season. These events often include the tasting of the first-pressed olive oil, known as olio nuovo, which is celebrated for its fresh, robust flavor. The communal nature of the olive harvest and the sharing of olive oil are expressions of the values of generosity, community, and connection to the land that are central to Italian culture.

The Olive Tree in Rituals and Religion

The olive tree has played a significant role in religious rituals and practices in the Mediterranean region for millennia. In ancient Greece, olive oil was used to anoint athletes, warriors, and kings, symbolizing strength, purity, and divine favor. The oil was also used in religious ceremonies, where it was burned in lamps to honor the gods and to light temples.

In Judaism, the olive tree is a symbol of beauty, fertility, and the connection between God and the people of Israel. Olive oil was used in the Temple in Jerusalem to light the menorah, the seven-branched candelabrum that symbolized the divine light of God. This use of olive oil in religious rituals has continued in Jewish tradition, where it is still used to light the menorah during the festival of Hanukkah.

In Christianity, the olive tree and its oil have similarly profound significance. The Garden of Gethsemane, where Jesus prayed before his arrest, was located on the Mount of Olives, a place that was covered with olive trees. The name "Gethsemane" itself means "oil press," reflecting the importance of olive cultivation in the region. Olive oil is used in many Christian sacraments, including baptism, confirmation, and the anointing of the sick, symbolizing the presence of the Holy Spirit and the healing power of God.

The use of olive oil in religious rituals underscores its symbolic value as a substance that bridges the human and the divine. In these traditions, the olive tree is seen as a sacred plant, one that connects people to the natural world and to the spiritual realm. The legend of the olive tree, with its origins in divine intervention, reinforces this connection and highlights the tree's role as a symbol of life, healing, and spiritual nourishment.

The Olive Tree as a Symbol of Resilience and Longevity

One of the most remarkable qualities of the olive tree is its resilience. Olive trees can live for hundreds, even thousands of *years, and they are capable of surviving in harsh conditions where other plants would wither and die. This resilience has made the olive tree a powerful symbol of endurance and longevity, qualities that are highly valued in Mediterranean culture.*

The gnarled trunks and twisted branches of ancient olive trees tell the story of survival through the ages. These trees have witnessed wars, famines, and the rise and fall of empires, yet they continue to stand, producing fruit year after year. In this way, the olive tree serves as a metaphor for the resilience of the people who have cultivated it, people who have faced their own hardships and yet have managed to endure and thrive.

In Italy, there are olive trees that are over a thousand years old, some of which have been designated as national monuments. These ancient trees are revered not only for their age but for their symbolic connection to the past. They are living links to the ancestors who planted and tended them, and they represent the continuity of life and tradition through the generations.

The longevity of the olive tree also ties into its symbolism as a tree of peace and reconciliation. Just as the tree can live for centuries, so too can the peace and stability that it represents. The tree's ability to regenerate, even after being cut back or damaged, symbolizes the potential for renewal and healing in human relationships. This idea is reflected in the practice of planting olive trees as a gesture of peace, a tradition that continues in various parts of the world today.

The Olive Tree in Italian Art and Literature

The olive tree has been a prominent motif in Italian art and literature for centuries. Its image has been used to convey themes of peace, wisdom, and connection to the land, and it has appeared in countless works of painting, sculpture, and poetry.

During the Italian Renaissance, the olive tree was often depicted in religious art, where it symbolized peace and divine favor. The tree appeared in scenes of the Annunciation, where the angel Gabriel announces to Mary that she will bear the Son of God, and in depictions of the Garden of Gethsemane, where Jesus prayed before his crucifixion. These works of art used the olive tree to convey the spiritual significance of the events they portrayed, linking the tree's natural beauty to the divine.

In Italian literature, the olive tree has been celebrated as a symbol of the countryside and the rural way of life. Poets and writers have used the tree as a metaphor for the enduring connection between people and the land, as well as for the values of hard work, resilience, and simplicity that characterize rural life. The olive tree has been a source of inspiration for poets such as Eugenio Montale and Salvatore Quasimodo, who have written about the tree's beauty and its significance in Italian culture.

The tree's symbolism extends beyond its visual and literary representations to its role in everyday life. The act of tending to olive trees, harvesting their fruit, and producing olive oil is itself a form of art, one that requires skill, patience, and a deep understanding of the land. In this way, the olive tree represents the fusion of nature and culture, where the cultivation of the tree is both a practical and an aesthetic pursuit.

The Olive Tree and Environmental Sustainability

In recent years, the olive tree has also come to symbolize environmental sustainability and the importance of preserving traditional agricultural practices. Olive cultivation, with its low impact on the environment and its ability to thrive in marginal lands, is seen as a model for sustainable agriculture in the Mediterranean region.

The deep-rooted nature of the olive tree helps to prevent soil erosion, and its ability to withstand drought makes it an important crop in areas where water is scarce. The tree's long lifespan means that it can provide a stable source of income for farmers over many generations, contributing to the economic sustainability of rural communities.

The production of olive oil, which has been practiced in the Mediterranean for thousands of years, is also a model of sustainability. Traditional methods of olive oil production, which involve hand-picking the olives and cold-pressing them to extract the oil, are environmentally friendly and produce high-quality oil with minimal waste. These methods have been passed down through generations, preserving both the quality of the oil and the cultural heritage associated with its production.

In Italy, there has been a growing movement to protect and promote traditional olive cultivation practices, particularly in the face of challenges such as climate change, urbanization, and the spread of diseases that threaten olive trees. Initiatives to protect ancient olive groves, promote organic farming methods, and support small-scale olive oil producers are all part of a broader effort to ensure that the olive tree continues to play a central role in Mediterranean life for generations to come.

Conclusion

The Legend of the Olive Tree is more than just a story; it is a reflection of the deep cultural, spiritual, and environmental significance of the olive tree in Italy and the Mediterranean region. The tree's resilience, its ability to provide sustenance, and its symbolism as a source of peace and wisdom have made it an enduring symbol in the region's history and culture.

Through its associations with the goddess Athena, the olive tree has come to represent the values of wisdom, peace, and prosperity. Its role in religious rituals and its use as a symbol of reconciliation further underscore its importance as a cultural and spiritual icon. The olive tree's presence in art and literature, as well as its central role in the Mediterranean diet, highlight its multifaceted significance in the lives of the people who have cultivated it for thousands of years.

In an era where sustainability and environmental stewardship are increasingly important, the olive tree also serves as a symbol of the enduring connection between humans and the natural world. Its ability to thrive in harsh conditions, its contribution to sustainable agriculture, and its role in preserving traditional practices make it a model for how we can live in harmony with the environment.

The legend of the olive tree, with its themes of resilience, peace, and connection to the land, continues to inspire and teach. It is a story that reminds us of the enduring power of nature, the importance of preserving our cultural heritage, and the timeless values that the olive tree represents. As long as olive trees continue to grow and flourish in the Mediterranean, the legend of the olive tree will remain a vital part of the cultural fabric of the region, connecting the past to the present and offering hope for the future.

The Magic Ring

In a small, sun-dappled village nestled among the rolling hills of Italy, there lived a young man named Pietro. Pietro was known throughout the village for his kindness and generosity, despite his humble circumstances. He lived in a modest cottage at the edge of the village, earning a meager living as a woodcutter. Though he had little in the way of material wealth, Pietro's heart was rich with compassion, and he was always willing to help his neighbors, whether it was by chopping firewood for an elderly widow or sharing his simple meals with a hungry traveler.

Pietro's life was simple, but it was not without its challenges. The work of a woodcutter was hard and unforgiving, and the winters in the hills could be harsh. Despite his best efforts, Pietro often found himself struggling to make ends meet. His clothes were worn and patched, his boots barely held together, and his small home needed repairs that he could not afford. Yet Pietro remained cheerful, believing that as long as he had his health and the love of his neighbors, he was richer than any king.

One day, as Pietro was returning home from the forest with a bundle of firewood slung over his shoulder, he came across an old beggar sitting by the side of the road. The beggar was thin and ragged, his face lined with the marks of a hard life. He held out a trembling hand to Pietro and asked for a bit of bread or a few coins.

Moved by the beggar's plight, Pietro immediately set down his load of firewood and reached into his pocket. He had only a few coins to his name, but without hesitation, he gave them to the old man. "It's not much," Pietro said with a gentle smile, "but I hope it will help you find something to eat."

The beggar looked at the coins in his hand, then up at Pietro with eyes that seemed to glimmer with an otherworldly light. "You are a kind soul," the beggar said in a voice that was unexpectedly strong. "Few would give away what little they have to help a stranger. For your generosity, I wish to give you something in return—something far more valuable than coins."

Before Pietro could protest, the beggar reached into the folds of his tattered cloak and pulled out a small, ornate ring. The ring was made of gold, intricately engraved with delicate patterns that seemed to shimmer in the fading light. At its center was a gemstone, a deep green emerald that sparkled with an inner fire.

"This is no ordinary ring," the beggar said as he placed it in Pietro's hand. "It is a magic ring, one that can grant you anything your heart desires. But beware, young man, for such power comes with great responsibility. Use it wisely, and it will bring you happiness. But if you let greed and ambition guide your actions, the ring's magic may turn against you."

Pietro stared at the ring, mesmerized by its beauty and the promise of what it could do. He had heard tales of magical objects in the old stories, but he had never imagined that he would come into possession of one himself. He looked up to thank the beggar, but to his astonishment, the old man had vanished, leaving no trace of his presence.

Bewildered but intrigued, Pietro slipped the ring onto his finger. It fit perfectly, as though it had been made just for him. As he continued his walk home, he couldn't help but wonder what he might do with such a powerful gift. The idea of wealth and comfort was tempting—after all, it would mean an end to his struggles and the chance to help his neighbors in ways he had never been able to before.

That night, as Pietro sat by the fire in his humble cottage, he turned the ring over in his hand, contemplating its power. He decided to test the ring's magic with a simple wish. "I wish for a loaf of bread," he said aloud, his voice tinged with both excitement and doubt.

No sooner had the words left his mouth than a loaf of fresh, warm bread appeared on the table before him. Pietro's eyes widened in amazement, and he quickly tore off a piece of the bread, savoring its rich, hearty flavor. The ring was indeed magical, just as the beggar had said.

Over the next few days, Pietro experimented with the ring, making small, harmless wishes to see the extent of its power. He wished for new boots, and a pair appeared at the foot of his bed. He wished for a patch for the roof of his cottage, and the next morning, he found the hole mended as if by a master craftsman. Each time, the ring granted his wish without hesitation, and Pietro marveled at the possibilities that lay before him.

As the days turned into weeks, Pietro's life began to change. The ring allowed him to acquire everything he had ever needed or wanted. His once-shabby cottage became a cozy, well-furnished home, his clothes were replaced with fine garments, and his pantry was always stocked with food. The villagers noticed the change in Pietro's circumstances and marveled at his sudden good fortune, though he never revealed the secret of the magic ring.

But while Pietro enjoyed the comforts that the ring provided, he never forgot the beggar's warning. He used the ring's magic to help his neighbors, wishing for warm blankets for the poor, food for the hungry, and medicine for the sick. The villagers praised Pietro for his generosity, and his reputation as a kind and caring man only grew.

However, as time went on, Pietro began to sense a growing unease in his heart. The more he used the ring, the more he noticed that each wish, while granted, seemed to carry a subtle but unsettling consequence. The loaf of bread that had tasted so delicious left him feeling strangely hollow afterward. The new boots, though sturdy and fine, pinched his feet in a way that his old ones never had. And though his cottage was now warm and comfortable, Pietro found that he no longer slept as soundly as he once had, his dreams troubled by strange, shadowy figures.

One day, as Pietro was walking through the village, he overheard a conversation between two of his neighbors. They were speaking in hushed tones, their faces drawn with worry. "Have you heard about old Signora Rossi?" one of them whispered. "She fell ill last week, and nothing seems to help. It's as if the very life is being drained out of her."

Pietro's heart sank at the news. Signora Rossi was one of the villagers he had helped with the ring's magic. He had wished for medicine to cure her ailments, and at first, it had seemed to work. But now, it appeared that something had gone wrong.

Troubled by the thought that his wish might have caused

more harm than good, Pietro rushed to Signora Rossi's home. He found the old woman lying in bed, her face pale and gaunt, her breathing shallow. Despite the efforts of the village healer, she seemed to be slipping away.

Pietro knelt beside her, guilt gnawing at him. "I'm so sorry," he whispered, though he couldn't bring himself to explain the true reason for his sorrow. He clasped her frail hand in his, silently wishing for her recovery, but the ring remained cold and unresponsive.

It was then that Pietro began to realize the true nature of the ring's magic. Though it could grant wishes, it did so in a way that was twisted and tainted, as if the power that fueled it was not entirely benevolent. The ring's magic had given him everything he had ever wanted, but it had also brought with it an undercurrent of darkness, a subtle curse that seemed to taint every wish he made.

Pietro knew that he had to find a way to rid himself of the ring, but he also knew that it would not be easy. The ring had become a part of him, its power intoxicating and difficult to resist. Yet he could not ignore the warning signs, the growing unease that told him that the longer he kept the ring, the greater the danger he would face.

And so, with a heavy heart, Pietro resolved to find a way to break the ring's hold over him and to undo the harm that had been done. But the path ahead would be fraught with challenges and temptations, and Pietro would need all the wisdom and courage he could muster to overcome them.

As Pietro struggled with the growing unease that the ring had brought into his life, he found himself increasingly conflicted. The ring had granted him wealth and comfort beyond anything he had ever imagined, but it had also brought with it a heavy burden. The subtle darkness that accompanied each wish made Pietro wary of using the ring, yet the temptation to continue was strong. After all, he had grown accustomed to the ease and prosperity that the ring had provided.

One evening, as Pietro sat by the fire in his now-luxurious cottage, he turned the ring over in his hands, his thoughts heavy with doubt. He knew he could not continue using the ring as he had been, but he also felt powerless to stop. The allure of the ring's magic was undeniable—it had the ability to grant him anything he desired, yet the consequences of those wishes were beginning to weigh heavily on his conscience.

As Pietro pondered his predicament, a soft knock came at his door. Surprised, he rose to answer it, wondering who might be visiting him at such a late hour. When he opened the door, he found a young woman standing on his doorstep, her face pale and her expression anxious. Pietro recognized her as Maria, the daughter of one of his neighbors.

"Pietro," Maria said, her voice trembling, "I need your help. My father is very ill, and nothing the healer has tried seems to work. I heard that you have a way of making things better... please, can you help him?"

Pietro's heart sank at Maria's plea. He had used the ring's magic to help others before, but the unsettling consequences had made him wary of doing so again. Yet how could he refuse Maria's request when she was so desperate for help?

Without a word, Pietro nodded and followed Maria to her home. When they arrived, he found Maria's father lying in bed, his face flushed with fever and his breathing labored. The sight of the ailing man filled Pietro with a deep sense of dread—he had seen this before, and he knew that the ring's magic could bring temporary relief, but at what cost?

With a heavy heart, Pietro slipped the ring onto his finger and silently wished for the man's recovery. He watched as the fever seemed to subside, the man's breathing steadying as he drifted into a peaceful sleep. Maria's eyes filled with tears of gratitude as she thanked Pietro profusely, but he could not shake the gnawing fear that something terrible would follow.

In the days that followed, the man's condition improved, and word spread through the village of Pietro's miraculous ability to heal the sick. People began to come to him with their ailments and troubles, asking for his help. Each time, Pietro hesitated, torn between his desire to help and his fear of the ring's dark power. But the pleas of his neighbors were hard to resist, and so, reluctantly, Pietro continued to use the ring, even as the sense of foreboding grew within him.

One evening, as Pietro returned home from another such visit, he found himself utterly exhausted, not just physically but emotionally. The weight of the ring's magic was becoming too much to bear. Each wish he made seemed to drain him of his vitality, leaving him feeling more and more disconnected from the life he once knew.

That night, as he lay in bed, Pietro was plagued by disturbing dreams. In his sleep, he saw visions of the ring—its golden band twisted and warped, the emerald at its center glowing with a malevolent light. He saw the faces of those he had helped, their expressions twisted in agony and despair, their voices calling out to him in anger and accusation. "You brought this upon us," they seemed to say. "You thought you were helping, but you only made things worse."

Pietro awoke with a start, his heart pounding in his chest. The darkness of the room seemed oppressive, and he could feel the weight of the ring on his finger like a shackle. He knew, without a doubt, that the ring was cursed—that its power was not a gift, but a trap designed to ensnare him.

Determined to rid himself of the ring once and for all, Pietro set out the next morning in search of a solution. He traveled to the nearby town, seeking out the wisdom of the local priest. The priest, an elderly man with a kind and gentle demeanor, listened patiently as Pietro recounted the tale of the ring and the troubling events that had followed its use.

"My son," the priest said after a long pause, "it is clear to me that this ring is no ordinary object. It may have been forged by dark forces, designed to tempt and corrupt those who seek to use its power. You must find a way to destroy it before it destroys you."

"But how?" Pietro asked, his voice filled with desperation. "The ring seems indestructible. I've tried to remove it, but it always finds its way back to me."

The priest nodded gravely. "There are some curses that cannot be easily broken. However, there is an old legend that speaks of a way to rid oneself of such a cursed object. It is said that the only way to break the curse is to return the ring to its place of origin—wherever it was first forged. Only by doing so can the dark magic be undone."

Pietro felt a glimmer of hope at the priest's words, but it was quickly overshadowed by uncertainty. "But how will I find where the ring came from? I was given it by a beggar, and I have no idea where it might have been forged."

The priest considered this for a moment. "The journey will not be easy, but you must follow the clues that the ring itself may provide. Often, cursed objects carry with them a trace of their origin—a memory, a vision, something that will guide you to where you need to go. You must be vigilant, and you must trust in the guidance of the Almighty."

Pietro thanked the priest and left the town, his mind filled with resolve. He knew that he had to embark on this journey, no matter how perilous it might be. The ring's curse was too dangerous to ignore, and he could not allow it to continue harming those around him.

As Pietro made his way back to the village, he began to notice subtle changes in the ring. The once-brilliant emerald seemed to have dimmed, its color now a murky green. The engravings on the band, which had once shimmered with an otherworldly light, now appeared faded and worn. It was as if the ring was weakening, its power diminishing as Pietro resolved to break its hold over him.

That night, as he slept, Pietro was visited by another dream—this one different from the nightmares that had plagued him before. In the dream, he saw a distant mountain, its peak shrouded in mist. At the base of the mountain was a cave, its entrance dark and foreboding. Pietro knew, instinctively, that this was the place he needed to find—the place where the ring had been forged.

The next morning, Pietro set out on his journey. He had no map, no clear direction, but the image of the mountain from his dream was etched in his mind. He traveled for days, through forests and over hills, always keeping the vision of the mountain in his thoughts.

As he traveled, Pietro encountered various challenges—storms that threatened to drive him off course, treacherous paths that tested his resolve, and strange, eerie sounds that seemed to follow him in the night. Yet despite these obstacles, Pietro pressed on, driven by the knowledge that he could not return home until he had freed himself from the ring's curse.

Finally, after what felt like an eternity of wandering, Pietro arrived at the foot of the mountain from his dream. The air was thick with mist, and the landscape was desolate, devoid of life. As he approached the cave, he felt a chill run down his spine. The entrance loomed before him, dark and ominous, as if it were the very mouth of the underworld.

Taking a deep breath, Pietro stepped into the cave, the darkness swallowing him whole. Inside, the air was cold and damp, and the walls were lined with strange, twisted shapes—stalactites and stalagmites that seemed to reach out like grasping hands. Pietro pressed on, the ring growing heavier with each step, its presence like a leaden weight on his soul.

At last, Pietro reached the heart of the cave, a vast chamber lit by a faint, eerie glow. In the center of the chamber was an ancient forge, long cold and abandoned, but still exuding a palpable sense of malevolent power. Pietro knew that this was the place—the place where the ring had been created.

With trembling hands, Pietro removed the ring from his finger and placed it on the anvil of the forge. He hesitated for a moment, the weight of the decision pressing down on him. But then, summoning all his strength, he raised a hammer he found nearby and brought it down with all his might.

The ring shattered into pieces, the sound echoing through the chamber like a thunderclap. For a moment, Pietro felt a surge of relief, but it was quickly followed by a sense of overwhelming exhaustion. The darkness of the cave seemed to close in around him, and he collapsed to the ground, unconscious.

When Pietro awoke, he found himself lying at the entrance of the cave, the morning sun shining down on him. The shattered pieces of the ring were gone, as if they had never existed. Pietro felt lighter, as though a great burden had been lifted from his shoulders. The curse had been broken, and the ring's dark power had been destroyed.

With a deep sense of gratitude and newfound clarity, Pietro made his way back to the village. He had learned a valuable lesson on his journey—a lesson about the dangers of greed, the corrupting influence of power, and the importance of living a simple, honest life. The magic ring, though it had offered him wealth and comfort, had nearly destroyed him, and he knew now that true happiness could only be found in the contentment of a humble, unburdened heart.

When Pietro returned to the village, he was greeted with joy by his neighbors, who had been worried about his sudden disappearance. Though they noticed that Pietro no longer possessed the riches and comforts he had once acquired, they also saw that he was at peace, free from the shadows that had darkened his life.

From that day on, Pietro lived simply, content with the modest life he had once led. He no longer sought wealth or power, but instead focused on helping others in small, meaningful ways. And in doing so, he found the true magic of life—the magic of kindness, generosity, and the quiet joy of knowing that he had made the world a better place.

Cultural Significance and Facts about The Magic Ring

The Magic Ring is a classic example of an Italian folk tale that explores themes of temptation, morality, and the human condition. This tale, like many others from Italy, is deeply rooted in the cultural and social contexts of the time, serving as a vehicle for imparting moral lessons and reflecting the values of the society in which it originated. The story of The Magic Ring is not just a fantastical narrative about a powerful object; it is a reflection of the timeless struggles between good and evil, the dangers of unchecked ambition, and the importance of humility and virtue. The tale resonates with the broader themes found in Italian folklore and provides insights into the cultural psyche of the people who told and retold these stories over generations.

The Role of Folk Tales in Italian Culture

Folk tales have always played a crucial role in Italian culture, serving as a means of passing down wisdom, moral lessons, and cultural values from one generation to the next. These stories were often told orally, passed down through families and communities, and were an integral part of the social fabric of rural Italy. In a society where literacy was not widespread, folk tales provided a way for people to make sense of the world around them, to understand the complexities of human nature, and to navigate the challenges of life.

The Magic Ring fits squarely within this tradition. It is a tale that warns of the dangers of greed and the corrupting influence of power, themes that are prevalent in many Italian folk stories. The story emphasizes the importance of leading a simple, honest life, a value that has been deeply ingrained in Italian culture, particularly in rural areas where life was often harsh and resources were scarce. Through the character of Pietro, the story illustrates the consequences of giving in to temptation and the ultimate realization that true happiness cannot be found in material wealth or power but in humility and integrity.

The Symbolism of the Magic Ring

The magic ring in the story serves as a powerful symbol, representing the allure of power and the dangers that come with it. In many cultures, rings are symbolic objects, often associated with power, authority, and eternal bonds. In Italian folklore, as well as in other European traditions, magical rings are common motifs, often depicted as objects that can grant wishes or confer great power upon their wearer. However, these rings are also frequently portrayed as double-edged swords—while they offer the promise of fulfilling desires, they often come with a curse or a heavy price.

In The Magic Ring, the ring embodies the idea that power can corrupt even the most well-intentioned individuals. Pietro, who starts as a kind-hearted and generous young man, is gradually drawn into the ring's power, tempted by the ease with which it can grant his wishes. The ring's magic is seductive, offering instant gratification and the ability to shape the world according to one's desires. However, as Pietro soon discovers, the ring's power is not benign. Each wish comes with unforeseen consequences, and the ring's magic begins to exert a dark influence over his life.

This portrayal of the magic ring reflects broader themes in Italian folklore and literature, where the pursuit of power is often depicted as fraught with peril. The ring serves as a cautionary *symbol, warning against the dangers of seeking control over others or the world without considering the ethical implications. It also highlights the idea that true power lies not in the ability to manipulate the external world but in mastering one's own desires and impulses.*

Moral Lessons and the Italian Cultural Context

The moral lessons embedded in The Magic Ring are reflective of the values that have shaped Italian culture, particularly in rural and traditional communities. One of the central themes of the story is the idea that wealth and power, when pursued for their own sake, lead to ruin rather than happiness. This is a common motif in Italian folk tales, where characters who seek material gain or supernatural powers often face dire consequences.

In Italy, particularly in the rural regions where these stories were most commonly told, life was often characterized by hard work, scarcity, and a close-knit community structure. In such an environment, the pursuit of individual wealth or power at the expense of others was viewed with suspicion and often condemned. The story of The Magic Ring reinforces the idea that those who seek to elevate themselves above their neighbors through dishonest or selfish means will ultimately suffer for their actions.

The tale also emphasizes the virtues of humility, generosity, and contentment. Pietro's journey—from a humble woodcutter to a man corrupted by the ring's power, and finally to someone who renounces that power—mirrors the cultural belief that true happiness is found in leading a life of moderation and integrity. The story suggests that those who remain true to these values, even in the face of temptation, will ultimately find peace and fulfillment.

This message is particularly resonant in the context of Italian

Catholicism, which has historically placed a strong emphasis on the dangers of avarice and the importance of humility. The story's moral arc, where Pietro learns to renounce the ring's power and return to a simpler, more virtuous life, aligns with the Catholic teachings on the perils of sin and the redemptive power of repentance.

The Influence of Italian Catholicism on the Tale

Italian folk tales often reflect the deep influence of Catholicism on the cultural and moral landscape of the country. The Magic Ring is no exception, as it incorporates elements that resonate with Christian teachings and values. The story's emphasis on the dangers of temptation, the importance of moral integrity, and the idea of redemption through humility all align with Catholic doctrine.

In many Italian folk tales, the intervention of divine or supernatural forces is a common theme. These forces often serve as agents of justice, rewarding the virtuous and punishing the wicked. In The Magic Ring, the old beggar who gives Pietro the ring can be seen as a test of Pietro's character. While the beggar's true nature is never fully revealed, his role in the story suggests a connection to the idea of divine testing—a common motif in Catholic teachings, where individuals are often tested by God or saints to prove their faith and moral fortitude.

The story's resolution, where Pietro ultimately destroys the ring and returns to a life of simplicity and virtue, can be interpreted as a form of redemption. In Catholic tradition, repentance and the renunciation of sin are key components of spiritual growth and salvation. Pietro's decision to rid himself of the ring and its corrupting influence reflects the Catholic belief in the possibility of redemption through sincere repentance and a return to a righteous path.

The Folk Tale as a Reflection of Social Dynamics

Beyond its moral and religious themes, The Magic Ring also serves as a reflection of the social dynamics and concerns of the time. The tale speaks to the anxieties surrounding social mobility and the disruption of traditional social hierarchies. In a society where class divisions were often rigid and opportunities for upward mobility were limited, the idea of a magic ring that could grant wealth and power would have been both tantalizing and unsettling.

The story explores the potential dangers of suddenly acquiring wealth and influence without the accompanying social responsibilities or moral grounding. Pietro's initial use of the ring to help others reflects a communal ethic, where wealth is shared for the common good. However, as the ring's power begins to corrupt him, the story illustrates the potential for individual greed to undermine social harmony.

This tension between individual ambition and communal values is a recurring theme in Italian folk tales. The stories often caution against the dangers of disrupting the social order, whether through the pursuit of forbidden knowledge, the use of magic, or the accumulation of wealth. The moral of The Magic Ring reinforces the idea that those who seek to elevate themselves above their community or who disregard the well-being of others will ultimately face negative consequences.

The Role of Magic and the Supernatural in Italian Folklore

Magic and the supernatural are central elements in many Italian folk tales, serving as both plot devices and symbolic representations of larger themes. In The Magic Ring, the ring itself is a magical object that embodies the dual nature of magic in folklore—its potential to both bless and curse, to grant wishes but also to corrupt.

Italian folklore is rich with stories of magical objects, from rings and amulets to enchanted mirrors and cursed relics. These objects are often portrayed as having a will of their own, capable of influencing the actions and fates of those who possess them. In this context, the magic ring in Pietro's story is not just a tool but a character in its own right, with its own intentions and powers that must be understood and navigated by the protagonist.

The portrayal of magic in Italian folk tales is often ambivalent. While it can provide solutions to seemingly insurmountable problems, it also carries the risk of unintended consequences. This ambivalence reflects a broader cultural attitude toward the supernatural—one that recognizes its power but also treats it with caution and respect. The magic in these stories is often seen as a reflection of the complexities and uncertainties of life, where actions have consequences that are not always immediately apparent.

The Enduring Appeal of the Tale

The story of The Magic Ring has endured for generations, continuing to captivate audiences with its blend of fantasy, moral lessons, and cultural resonance. Its themes are timeless, *addressing universal human concerns such as the dangers of temptation, the corrupting influence of power, and the search for true happiness.*

The tale's enduring appeal lies in its ability to speak to different audiences on multiple levels. For children, it is an exciting story of magic and adventure, filled with the wonder of a powerful ring that can grant wishes. For adults, it is a more complex narrative that explores the moral and ethical dilemmas associated with power and wealth, as well as the importance of maintaining one's integrity in the face of temptation.

In modern times, the story continues to be relevant, particularly in a world where material wealth and the pursuit of power are often seen as measures of success. The Magic Ring serves as a reminder that true fulfillment cannot be found in external possessions or status, but in leading a life that is true to one's values and principles.

The tale also reflects the importance of community and the idea that individual actions have a broader impact on society. Pietro's journey teaches that while magic and power may offer temporary solutions, they can never replace the deeper satisfaction that comes from living in harmony with others and with oneself.

Conclusion

The Magic Ring is a rich and multifaceted folk tale that offers valuable insights into Italian culture, values, and the human condition. Through its exploration of themes such as temptation, power, and morality, the story provides a timeless lesson on the dangers of greed and the importance of humility and virtue.

The magic ring itself serves as a powerful symbol of the dual nature of power—its ability to grant wishes and fulfill desires, but also its potential to corrupt and destroy. The story's resolution, where Pietro learns to renounce the ring's power and return to a life of simplicity and integrity, reflects the cultural and moral values that have shaped Italian society for generations.

As a piece of Italian folklore, The Magic Ring continues to resonate with audiences today, offering a compelling narrative that speaks to the complexities of human nature and the timeless struggle between good and evil. Its enduring appeal lies in its ability to convey deep moral truths through the medium of fantasy, making it a story that will continue to be told and cherished for generations to come.

Epilogue

As the final page of this collection turns, we bid farewell to the enchanting world of Italian folklore, where magic breathes life into ancient hills and legends whisper through time. These tales, woven from the dreams and fears of generations past, are more than just stories—they are the threads that connect us to a shared cultural heritage, a reminder that the past lives on in every word, every myth, every echo of the voices that first told them.

In this journey through the mysteries of Italy's folk traditions, we have encountered heroes who defied the impossible, beings of magic who both blessed and cursed, and spirits who linger in the places where history and myth entwine. Each tale carries with it a piece of the land from which it sprang, a land where olive trees bear the weight of centuries and the dance of the tarantella pulses with the energy of life itself.

These stories are not just relics of the past; they are living entities, continually evolving as they are retold and reimagined by each new generation. As you close this book, remember that the magic within these pages is not confined to ink and paper. It is a part of the air we breathe, the landscapes we traverse, and the stories we share with one another.

May the legends of La Befana, Colapesce, Saint Agatha, and all the other characters you've met here stay with you, their lessons and wonders lingering in your heart. And as you go forth, may you carry with you the spirit of these tales—a belief in the extraordinary, an appreciation for the wisdom of old, and the courage to seek out the magic that still exists in the world around us.

Thank you for joining me on this journey. May these stories inspire you to look deeper, to listen closer, and to find the extraordinary in the everyday. Until we meet again in another volume, where more tales await to be discovered and shared, I wish you fair winds, bright days, and endless wonder.

Arrivederci, until the next story.

THE END

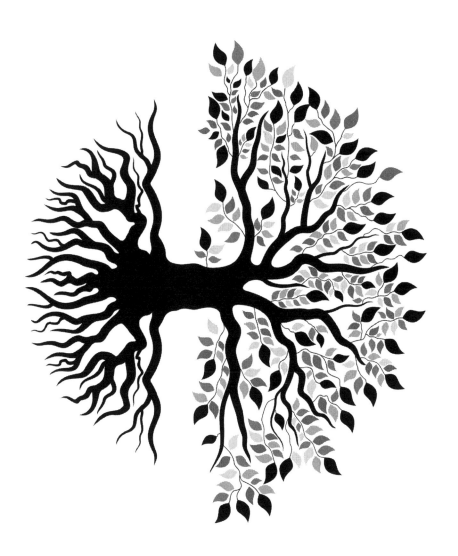

Join Our Enchanted Community!

Loved these timeless tales of magic and wonder? The adventure doesn't have to end here! Join our enchanted community and stay connected with a world of folklore, fairy tales, and much more.

By signing up for our mailing list, you'll receive:

Exclusive Updates: Be the first to know about upcoming releases, special editions, and new collections of folk tales from around the world.

Behind-the-Scenes Content: Discover the fascinating history and cultural insights behind your favorite stories.

Special Offers: Enjoy exclusive discounts, giveaways, and promotions available only to our subscribers.

Bonus Stories: Receive additional tales and magical content delivered straight to your inbox.

Don't miss out on the magic! **Scan the QR code below** to join our mailing list and embark on even more adventures.

Keep the stories alive, share the enchantment, and let the journey continue!

With warmest wishes,
The Folk Tales Team

Made in the USA
Columbia, SC
10 December 2024